H. G. Wells

THE WAR OF THE WORLDS

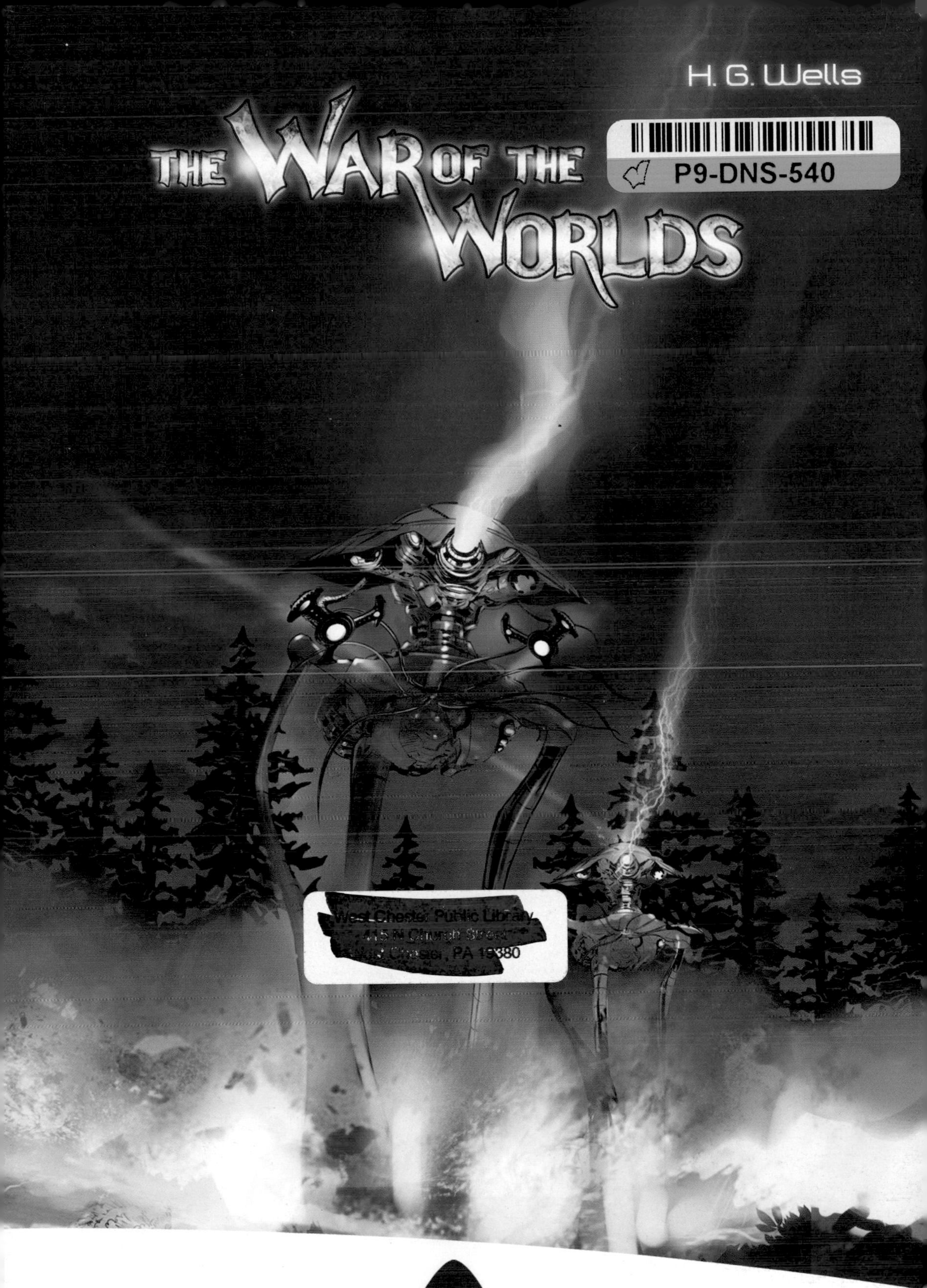

CAMPFIRE™

KALYANI NAVYUG MEDIA PVT. LTD.
New Delhi

THE WAR OF THE WORLDS

Sitting around the Campfire, telling the story, were:

WORDSMITH **RYAN FOLEY**

ILLUSTRATOR **BHUPENDRA AHLUWALIA**

COLORISTS **AKHIL P. LAL & PRADEEP SHERAWAT**

LETTERER **BHAVNATH CHAUDHARY**

EDITORS **SUPARNA DEB & ADITI RAY**

EDITOR (INFORMATIVE CONTENT) **RASHMI MENON**

PRODUCTION CONTROLLER **VISHAL SHARMA**

COVER ART & DESIGN **JAYAKRISHNAN K. P.**

www.campfire.co.in

Published by Kalyani Navyug Media Pvt. Ltd.
101 C, Shiv House, Hari Nagar Ashram, New Delhi 110014, India

ISBN: 978-93-80028-60-6

Printed in India at Tara Art Printers Pvt. Ltd.

ABOUT THE AUTHOR

Considered one of the pioneers of science fiction, Herbert George Wells was born on September 21, 1866 in England. He was the son of domestic servants who later became shopkeepers. Wells always had a great passion for reading, but with his family struggling to make ends meet, he spent much of his youth shuttling between school and a series of odd jobs. He did everything from working as an apprentice to a draper, to acting as an assistant to a chemist.

At the age of eighteen, Wells joined The Normal School of Science in Kensington to study Biology. Here he was taught by T. H. Huxley. This was a crucial period of his life as it had an immense influence on his writing.

Wells received a Bachelor of Science degree from the University of London in 1888, and began to teach. He enjoyed writing stories and articles alongside his day job, and gradually moved into writing on a full-time basis. He married his cousin Isabel Mary Wells in 1891.

The year 1895 was a turning point for Wells, both personally and professionally. It was the year he left his first wife and married a former student, Amy Catherine Robbins. It was also the year when his first major novel, *The Time Machine*, was published.

Still considered one of the greatest science fiction novels of all time, *The Time Machine* was the first in a string of successful books in which Wells's unique take on unusual subjects came to define certain genres. His tales of alien invasion in *The War of the Worlds*, invisibility in *The Invisible Man*, and eugenics in *The Island of Doctor Moreau* have influenced generations of writers.

While most famous for his work in science fiction, Wells worked on a variety of genres. An advocate of social change and member of the British socialist group, the Fabian Society, Wells spent much of his later years writing about his views on politics and society, and even offered predictions about the direction in which the world was headed. H.G. Wells continued writing until his death at the age of seventy-nine in 1946.

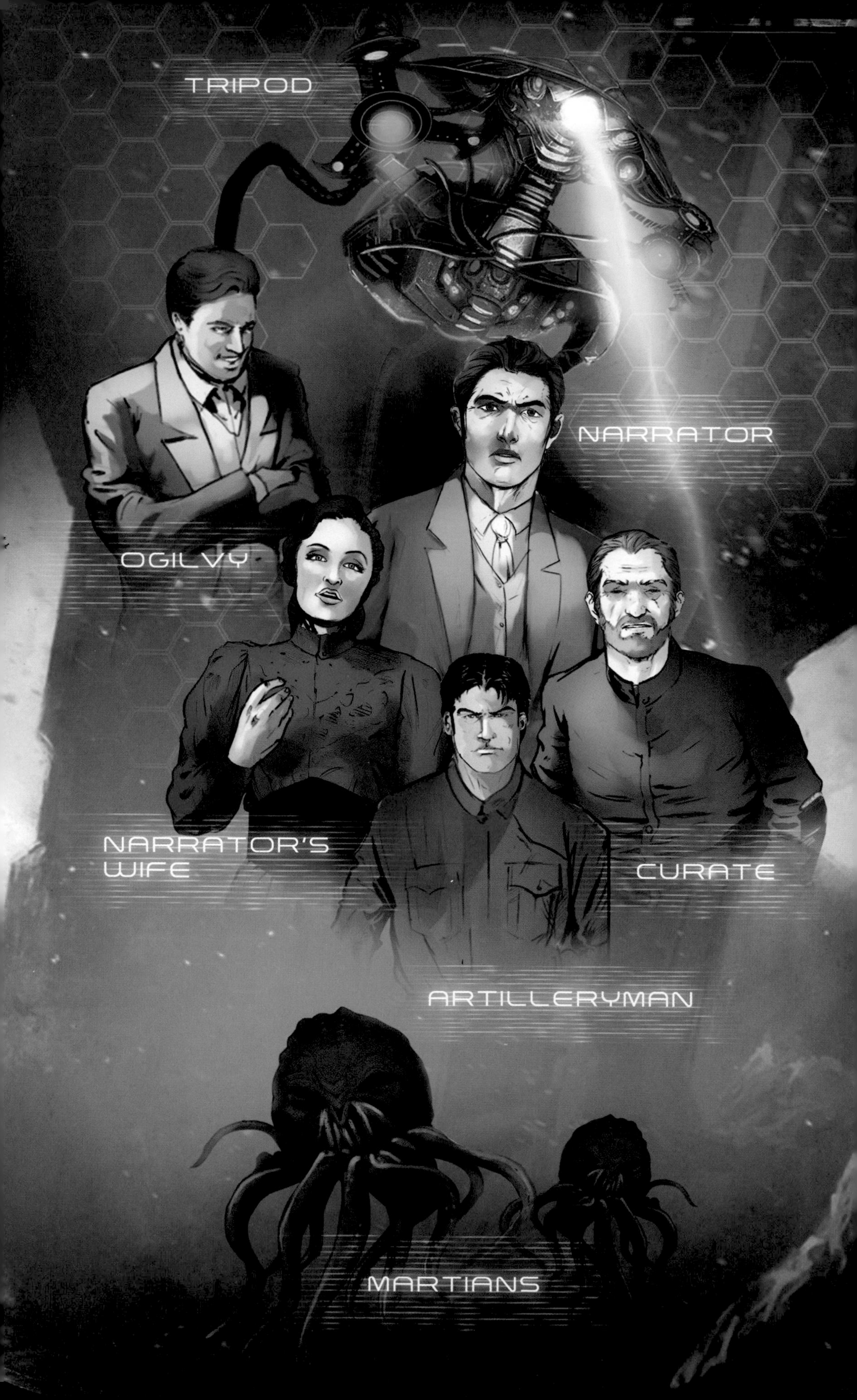
TRIPOD
NARRATOR
OGILVY
NARRATOR'S
WIFE
CURATE
ARTILLERYMAN
MARTIANS

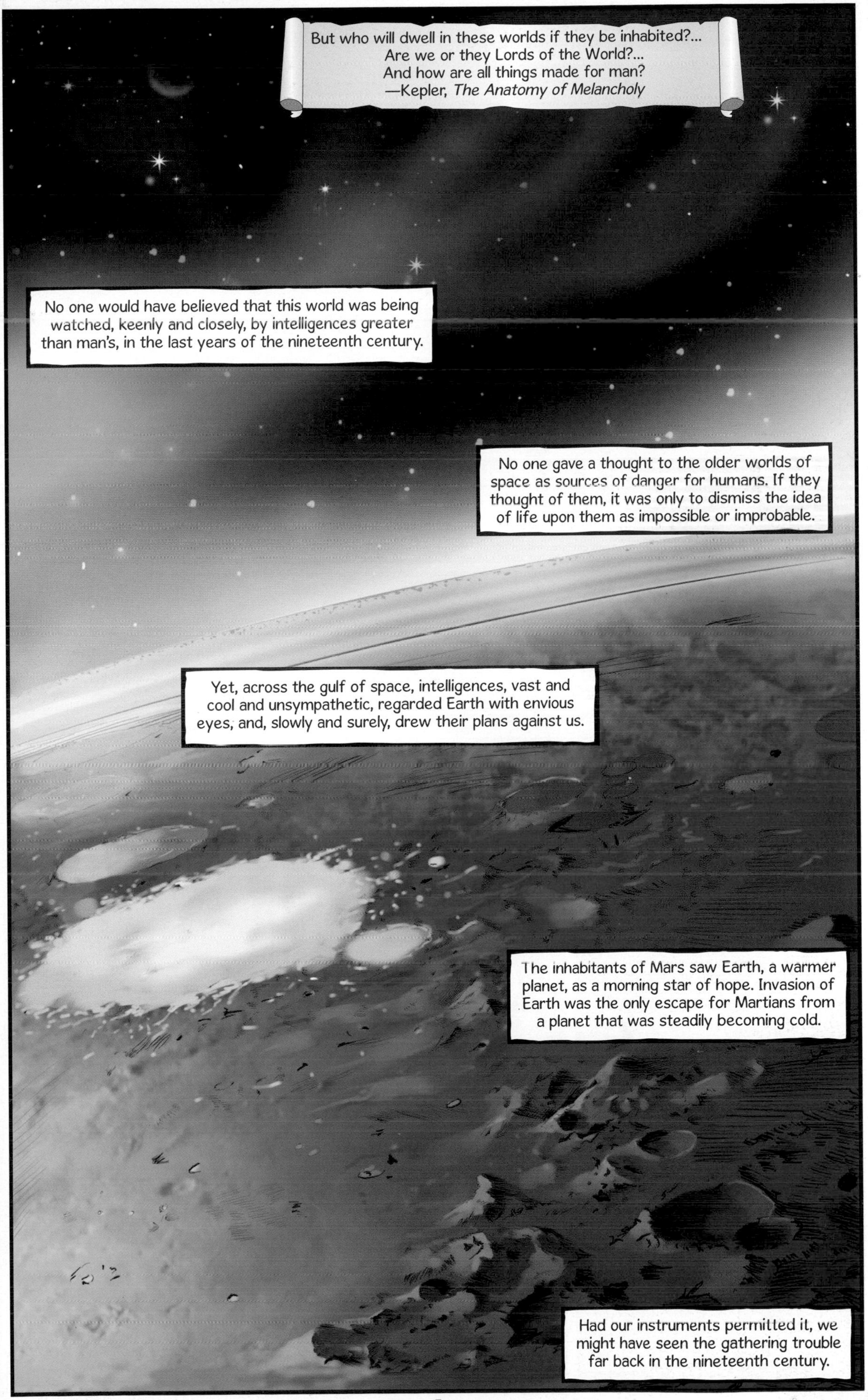
But who will dwell in these worlds if they be inhabited?... Are we or they Lords of the World?... And how are all things made for man? —Kepler, *The Anatomy of Melancholy*
No one would have believed that this world was being watched, keenly and closely, by intelligences greater than man's, in the last years of the nineteenth century.
No one gave a thought to the older worlds of space as sources of danger for humans. If they thought of them, it was only to dismiss the idea of life upon them as impossible or improbable.
Yet, across the gulf of space, intelligences, vast and cool and unsympathetic, regarded Earth with envious eyes, and, slowly and surely, drew their plans against us.
The inhabitants of Mars saw Earth, a warmer planet, as a morning star of hope. Invasion of Earth was the only escape for Martians from a planet that was steadily becoming cold.
Had our instruments permitted it, we might have seen the gathering trouble far back in the nineteenth century.

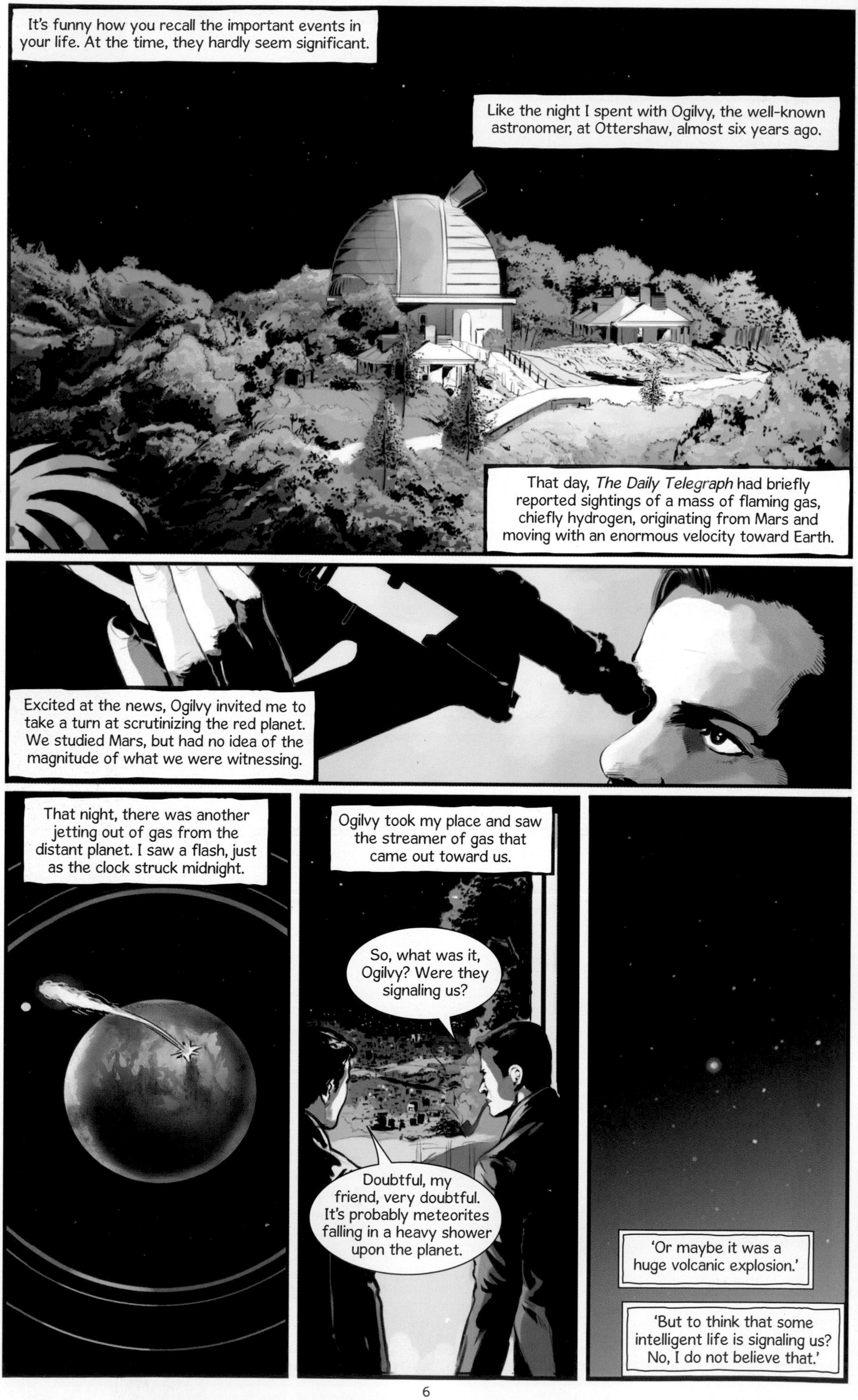
It's funny how you recall the important events in your life. At the time, they hardly seem significant.
Like the night I spent with Ogilvy, the well-known astronomer, at Ottershaw, almost six years ago.
That day, *The Daily Telegraph* had briefly reported sightings of a mass of flaming gas, chiefly hydrogen, originating from Mars and moving with an enormous velocity toward Earth.
Excited at the news, Ogilvy invited me to take a turn at scrutinizing the red planet. We studied Mars, but had no idea of the magnitude of what we were witnessing.
That night, there was another jetting out of gas from the distant planet. I saw a flash, just as the clock struck midnight.
Ogilvy took my place and saw the streamer of gas that came out toward us.
So, what was it, Ogilvy? Were they signaling us?
Doubtful, my friend, very doubtful. It's probably meteorites falling in a heavy shower upon the planet.
'Or maybe it was a huge volcanic explosion.'
'But to think that some intelligent life is signaling us? No, I do not believe that.'

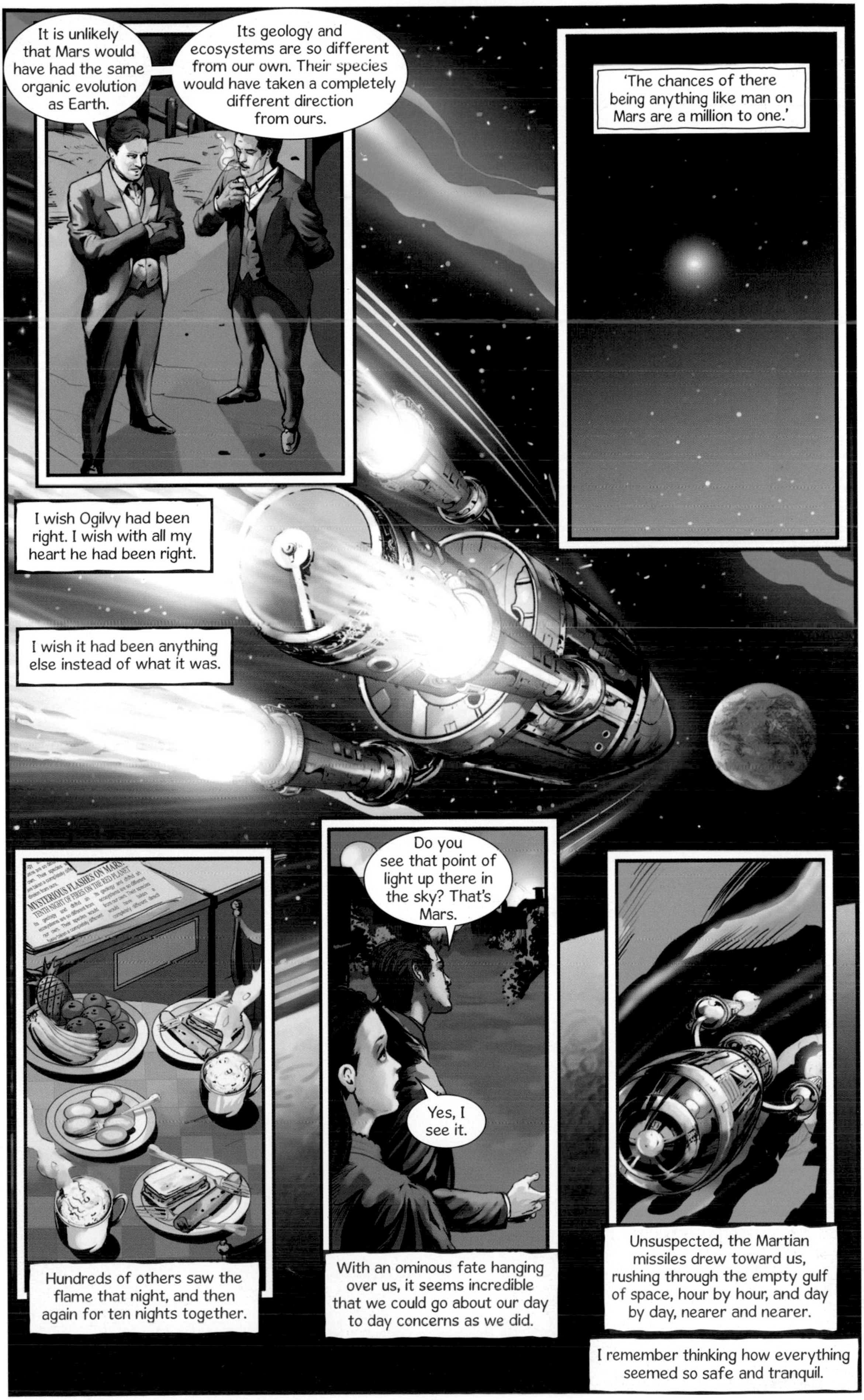
It is unlikely that Mars would have had the same organic evolution as Earth.
Its geology and ecosystems are so different from our own. Their species would have taken a completely different direction from ours.
'The chances of there being anything like man on Mars are a million to one.'
I wish Ogilvy had been right. I wish with all my heart he had been right.
I wish it had been anything else instead of what it was.
MYSTERIOUS FLASHES ON MARS
TENTH NIGHT OF FIRES ON THE RED PLANET
Hundreds of others saw the flame that night, and then again for ten nights together.
Do you see that point of light up there in the sky? That's Mars.
Yes, I see it.
With an ominous fate hanging over us, it seems incredible that we could go about our day to day concerns as we did.
Unsuspected, the Martian missiles drew toward us, rushing through the empty gulf of space, hour by hour, and day by day, nearer and nearer.
I remember thinking how everything seemed so safe and tranquil.

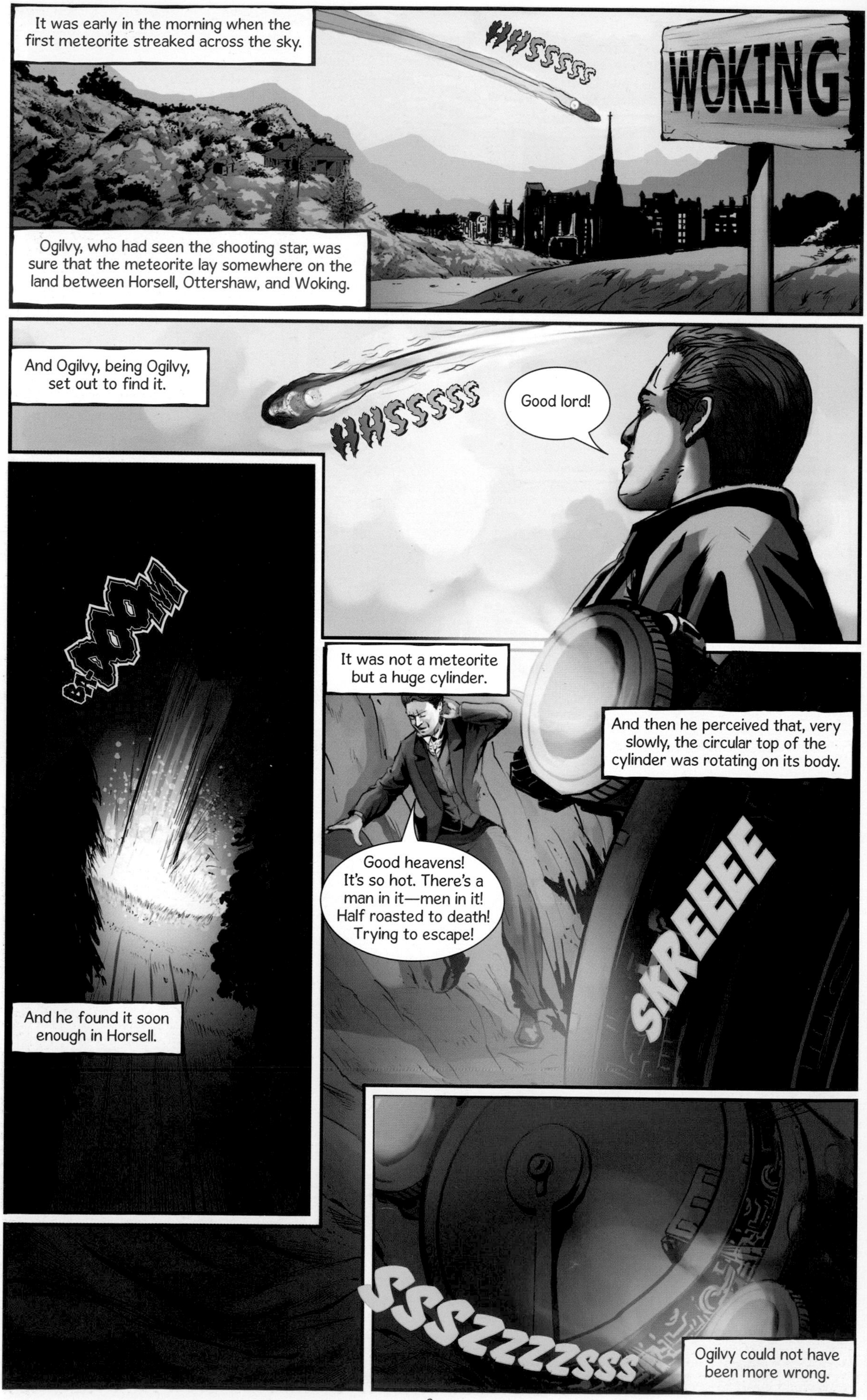

It was early in the morning when the first meteorite streaked across the sky.
WOKING
Ogilvy, who had seen the shooting star, was sure that the meteorite lay somewhere on the land between Horsell, Ottershaw, and Woking.
And Ogilvy, being Ogilvy, set out to find it.
Good lord!
And he found it soon enough in Horsell.
It was not a meteorite but a huge cylinder.
Good heavens! It's so hot. There's a man in it—men in it! Half roasted to death! Trying to escape!
And then he perceived that, very slowly, the circular top of the cylinder was rotating on its body.
Ogilvy could not have been more wrong.

News of Ogilvy's discovery spread like wildfire.

People came from all around to see 'the dead men from Mars'. It hit the local telegraph service, and the news traveled to London.

Good lord! It's true... Martians?

I lost no time in going across the Ottershaw Bridge to the sand pit, where the cylinder lay.

Alien Crash?

The Birmingham Daily Post.

A Message Received From Mars

The Daily News

Remarkable Story From Woking

The early editions of the evening papers carried enormous headlines of the incident.

As the day grew long, more and more people came to witness the strange occurrence in our quiet little town.

Ow! That's my foot!

Hey, let me see it!

Keep back!

Hey, move it!

By the time the sun started to set, a great crowd had gathered around the pit.

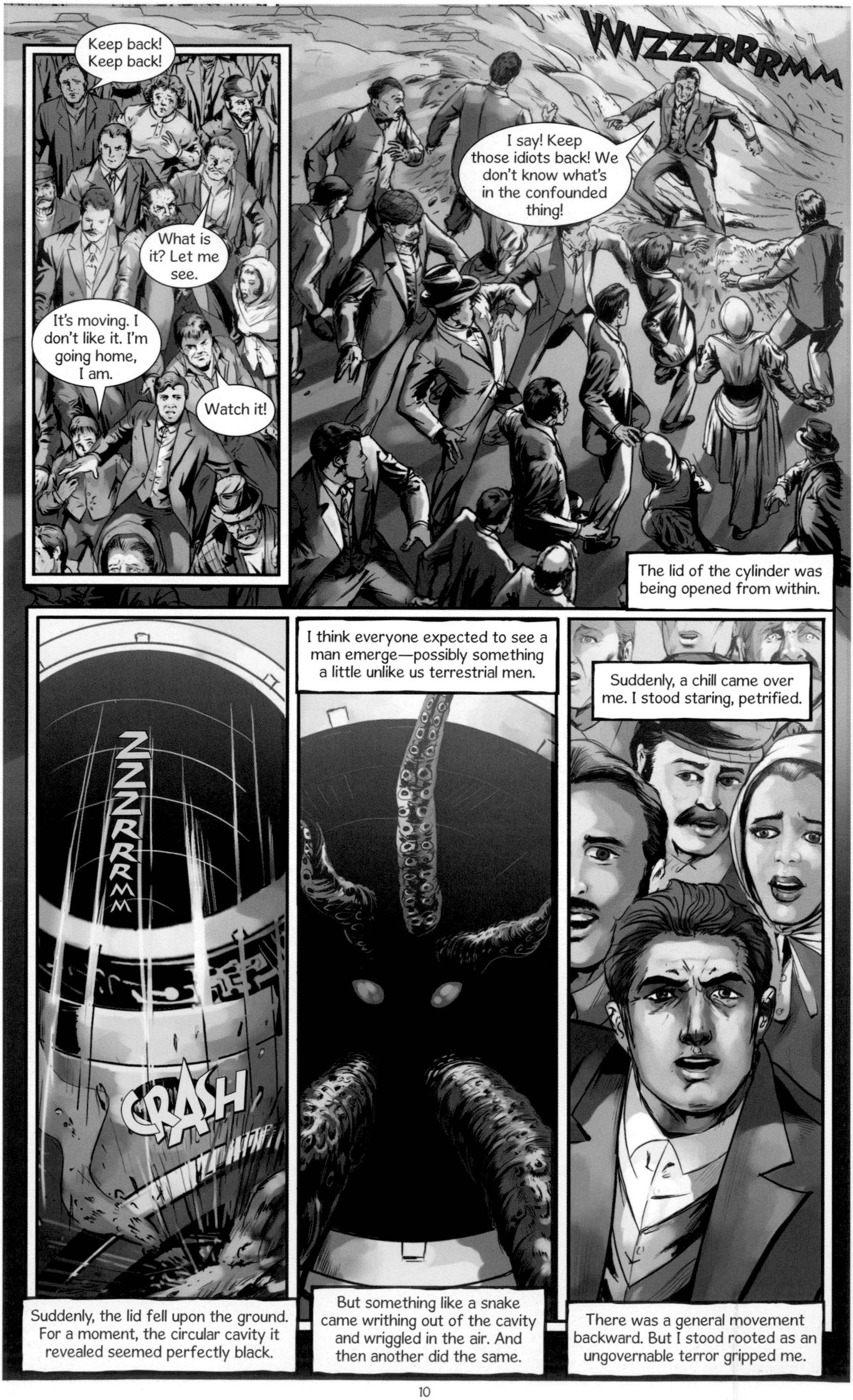
Keep back! Keep back!
What is it? Let me see.
It's moving. I don't like it. I'm going home, I am.
Watch it!
VVVZZZRRRRMM
I say! Keep those idiots back! We don't know what's in the confounded thing!
The lid of the cylinder was being opened from within.
ZZZRRRRMM
CRASH
Suddenly, the lid fell upon the ground. For a moment, the circular cavity it revealed seemed perfectly black.
I think everyone expected to see a man emerge—possibly something a little unlike us terrestrial men.
But something like a snake came writhing out of the cavity and wriggled in the air. And then another did the same.
Suddenly, a chill came over me. I stood staring, petrified.
There was a general movement backward. But I stood rooted as an ungovernable terror gripped me.

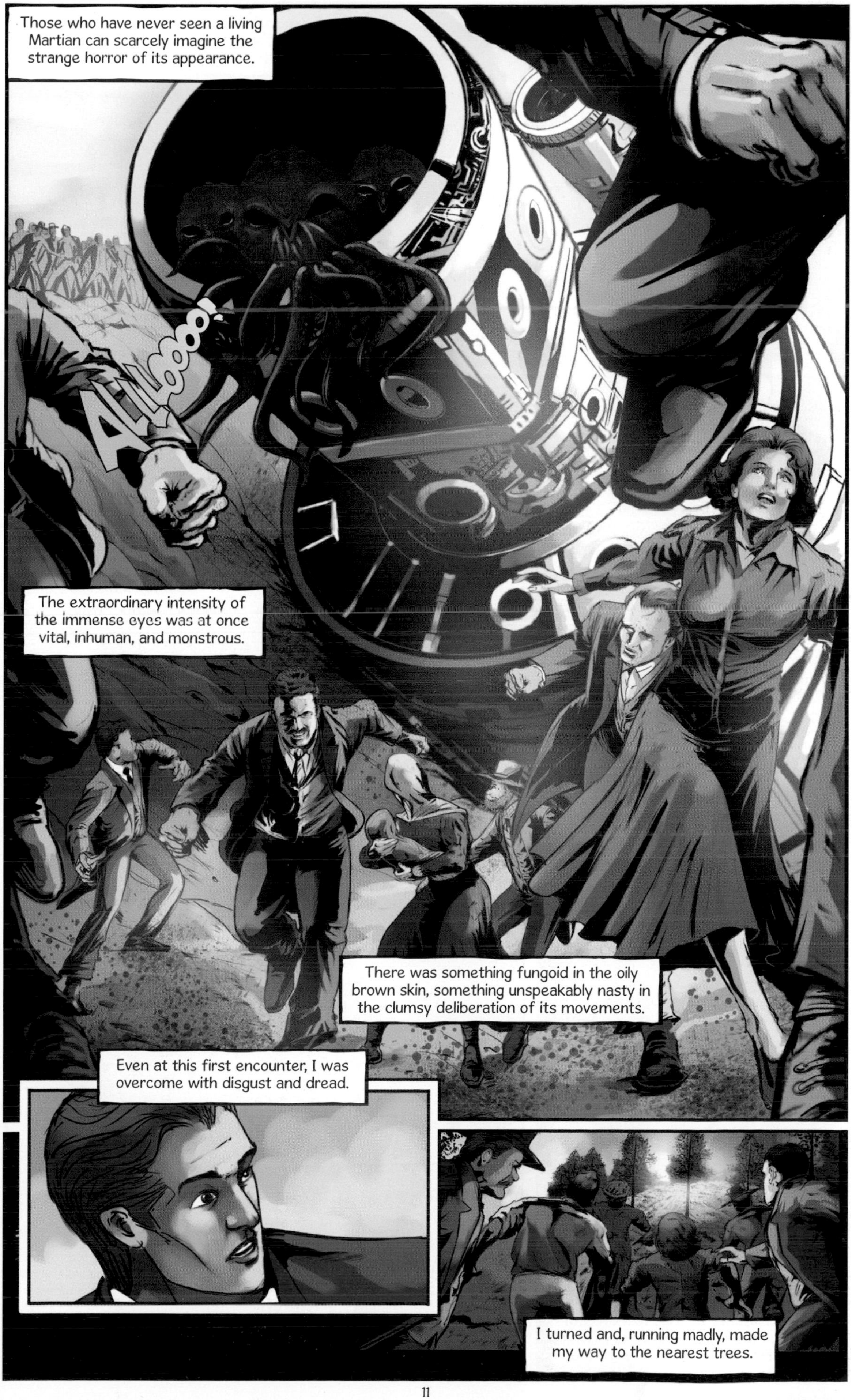
Those who have never seen a living Martian can scarcely imagine the strange horror of its appearance.
AULLOOOO!
The extraordinary intensity of the immense eyes was at once vital, inhuman, and monstrous.
There was something fungoid in the oily brown skin, something unspeakably nasty in the clumsy deliberation of its movements.
Even at this first encounter, I was overcome with disgust and dread.
I turned and, running madly, made my way to the nearest trees.

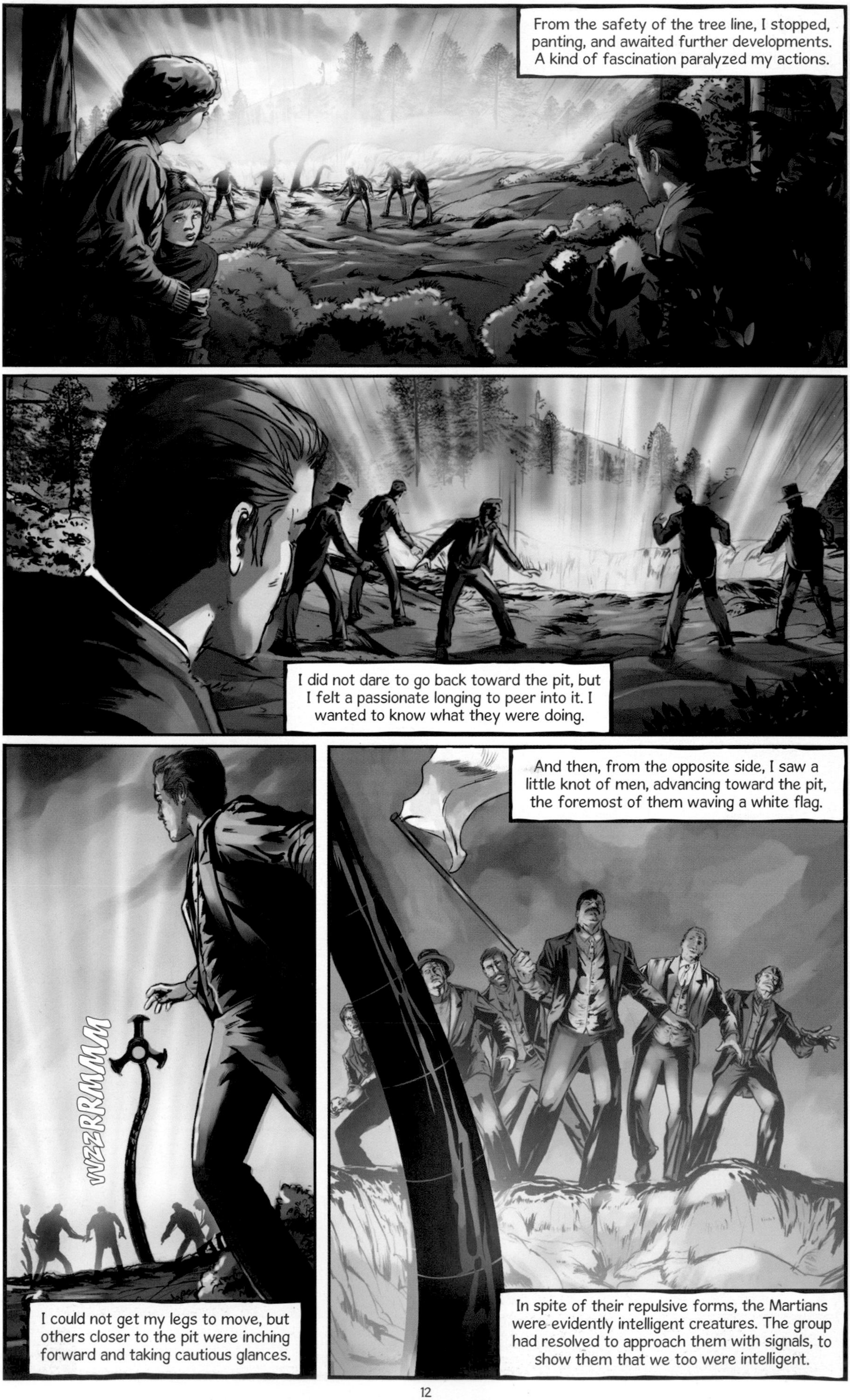
From the safety of the tree line, I stopped, panting, and awaited further developments. A kind of fascination paralyzed my actions.
I did not dare to go back toward the pit, but I felt a passionate longing to peer into it. I wanted to know what they were doing.
WZZRRMMM
I could not get my legs to move, but others closer to the pit were inching forward and taking cautious glances.
And then, from the opposite side, I saw a little knot of men, advancing toward the pit, the foremost of them waving a white flag.
In spite of their repulsive forms, the Martians were evidently intelligent creatures. The group had resolved to approach them with signals, to show them that we too were intelligent.

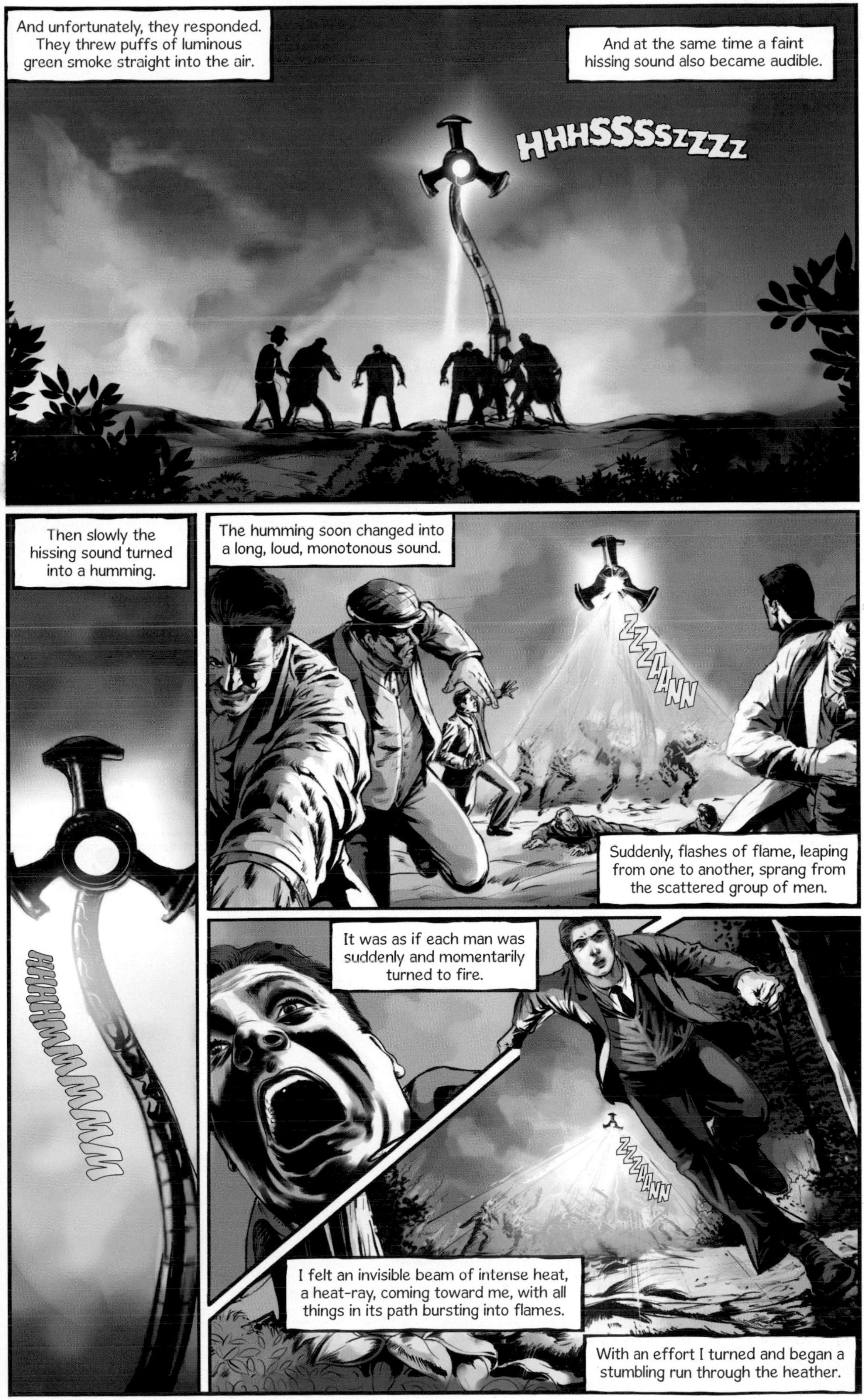

And unfortunately, they responded. They threw puffs of luminous green smoke straight into the air.
And at the same time a faint hissing sound also became audible.
HHHSSSSzzzz
Then slowly the hissing sound turned into a humming.
The humming soon changed into a long, loud, monotonous sound.
ZZZAANN
Suddenly, flashes of flame, leaping from one to another, sprang from the scattered group of men.
It was as if each man was suddenly and momentarily turned to fire.
ZZZAANN
I felt an invisible beam of intense heat, a heat-ray, coming toward me, with all things in its path bursting into flames.
With an effort I turned and began a stumbling run through the heather.

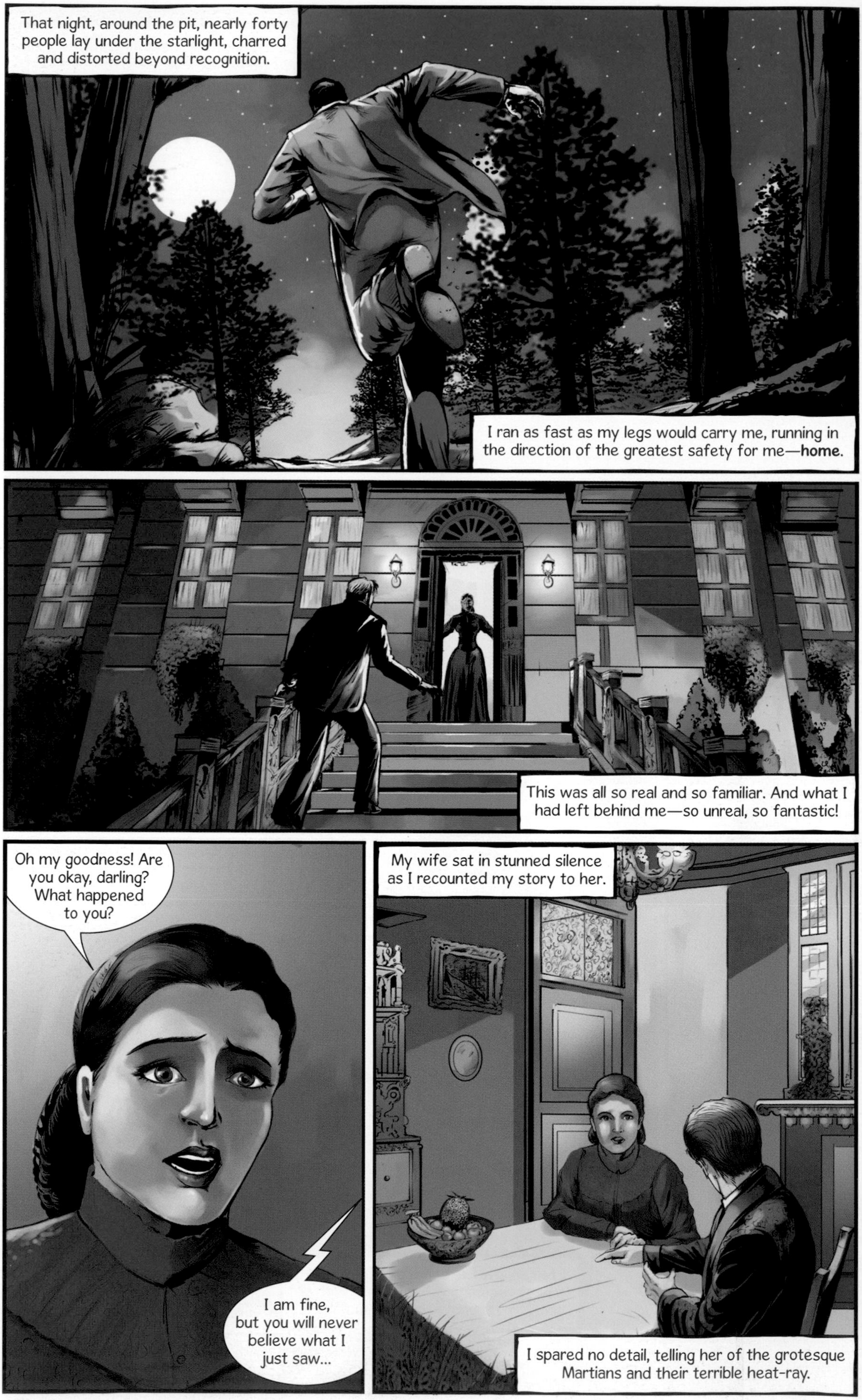
That night, around the pit, nearly forty people lay under the starlight, charred and distorted beyond recognition.
I ran as fast as my legs would carry me, running in the direction of the greatest safety for me—**home**.
This was all so real and so familiar. And what I had left behind me—so unreal, so fantastic!
Oh my goodness! Are you okay, darling? What happened to you?
I am fine, but you will never believe what I just saw...
My wife sat in stunned silence as I recounted my story to her.
I spared no detail, telling her of the grotesque Martians and their terrible heat-ray.

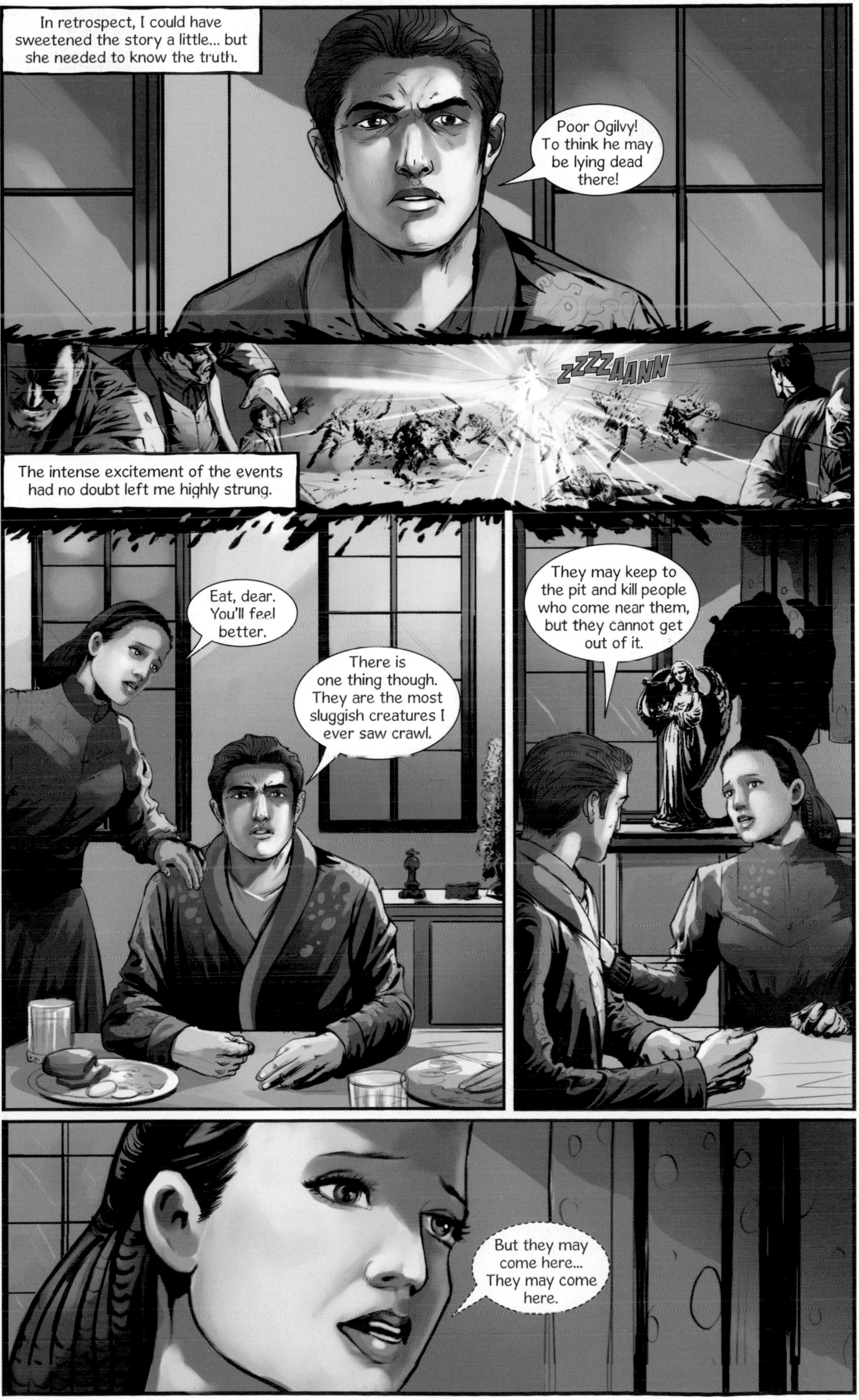
In retrospect, I could have sweetened the story a little... but she needed to know the truth.
Poor Ogilvy! To think he may be lying dead there!
ZZZZAANN
The intense excitement of the events had no doubt left me highly strung.
Eat, dear. You'll feel better.
There is one thing though. They are the most sluggish creatures I ever saw crawl.
They may keep to the pit and kill people who come near them, but they cannot get out of it.
But they may come here... They may come here.

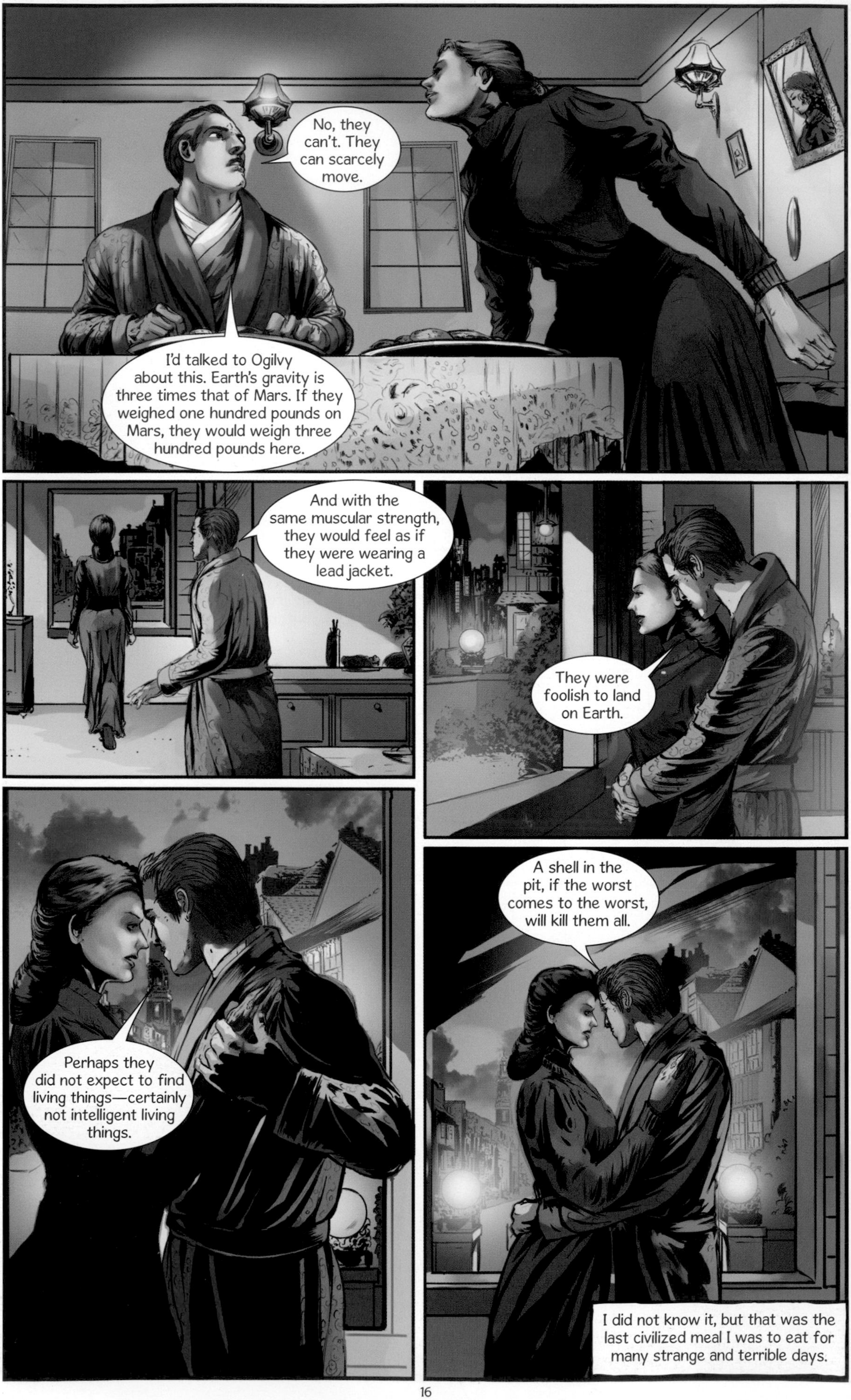
No, they can't. They can scarcely move.
I'd talked to Ogilvy about this. Earth's gravity is three times that of Mars. If they weighed one hundred pounds on Mars, they would weigh three hundred pounds here.
And with the same muscular strength, they would feel as if they were wearing a lead jacket.
They were foolish to land on Earth.
Perhaps they did not expect to find living things—certainly not intelligent living things.
A shell in the pit, if the worst comes to the worst, will kill them all.
I did not know it, but that was the last civilized meal I was to eat for many strange and terrible days.

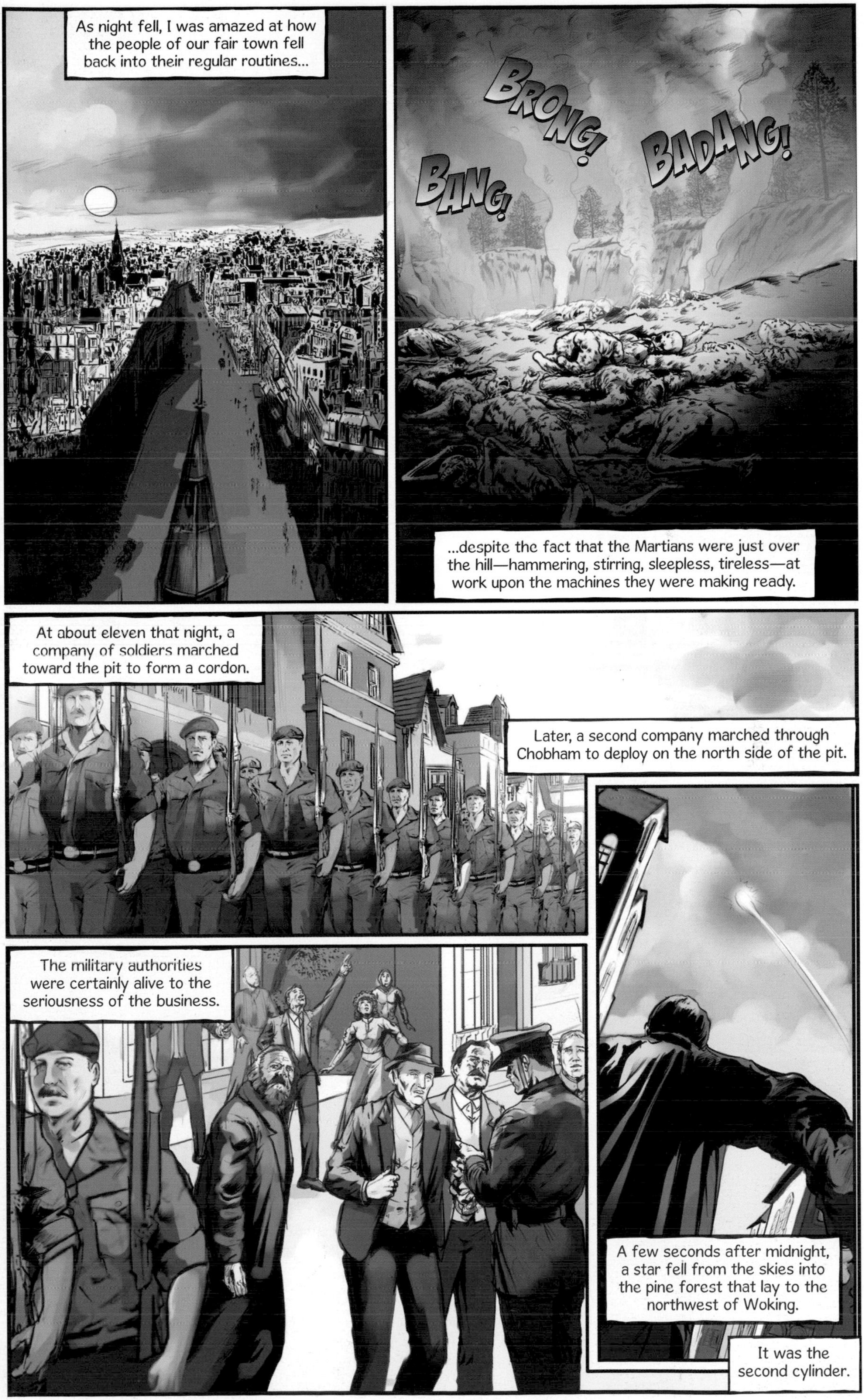
As night fell, I was amazed at how the people of our fair town fell back into their regular routines...
BRONG!
BADANG!
BANG!
...despite the fact that the Martians were just over the hill—hammering, stirring, sleepless, tireless—at work upon the machines they were making ready.
At about eleven that night, a company of soldiers marched toward the pit to form a cordon.
Later, a second company marched through Chobham to deploy on the north side of the pit.
The military authorities were certainly alive to the seriousness of the business.
A few seconds after midnight, a star fell from the skies into the pine forest that lay to the northwest of Woking.
It was the second cylinder.

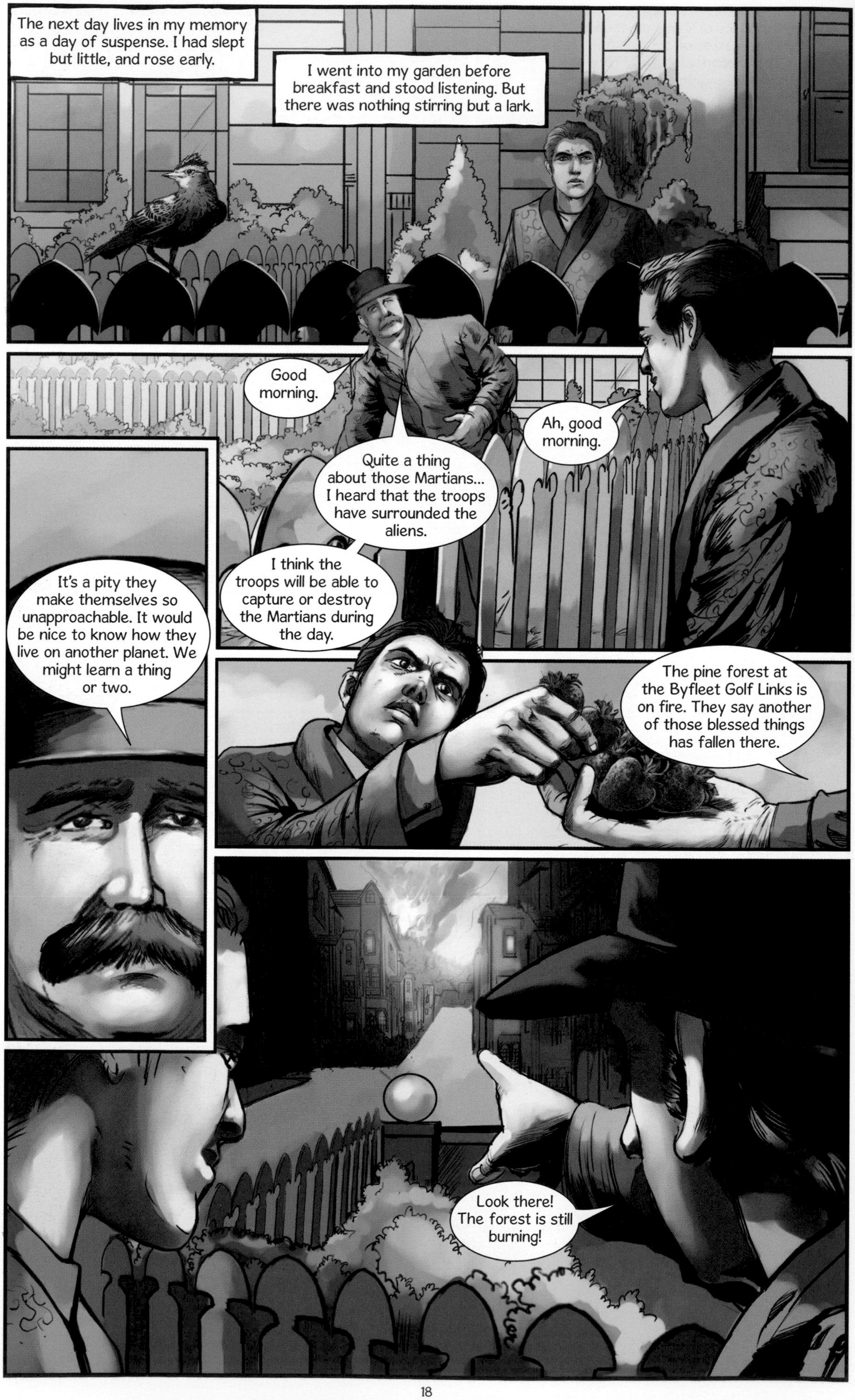
The next day lives in my memory as a day of suspense. I had slept but little, and rose early.
I went into my garden before breakfast and stood listening. But there was nothing stirring but a lark.
Good morning.
Ah, good morning.
Quite a thing about those Martians... I heard that the troops have surrounded the aliens.
I think the troops will be able to capture or destroy the Martians during the day.
It's a pity they make themselves so unapproachable. It would be nice to know how they live on another planet. We might learn a thing or two.
The pine forest at the Byfleet Golf Links is on fire. They say another of those blessed things has fallen there.
Look there! The forest is still burning!

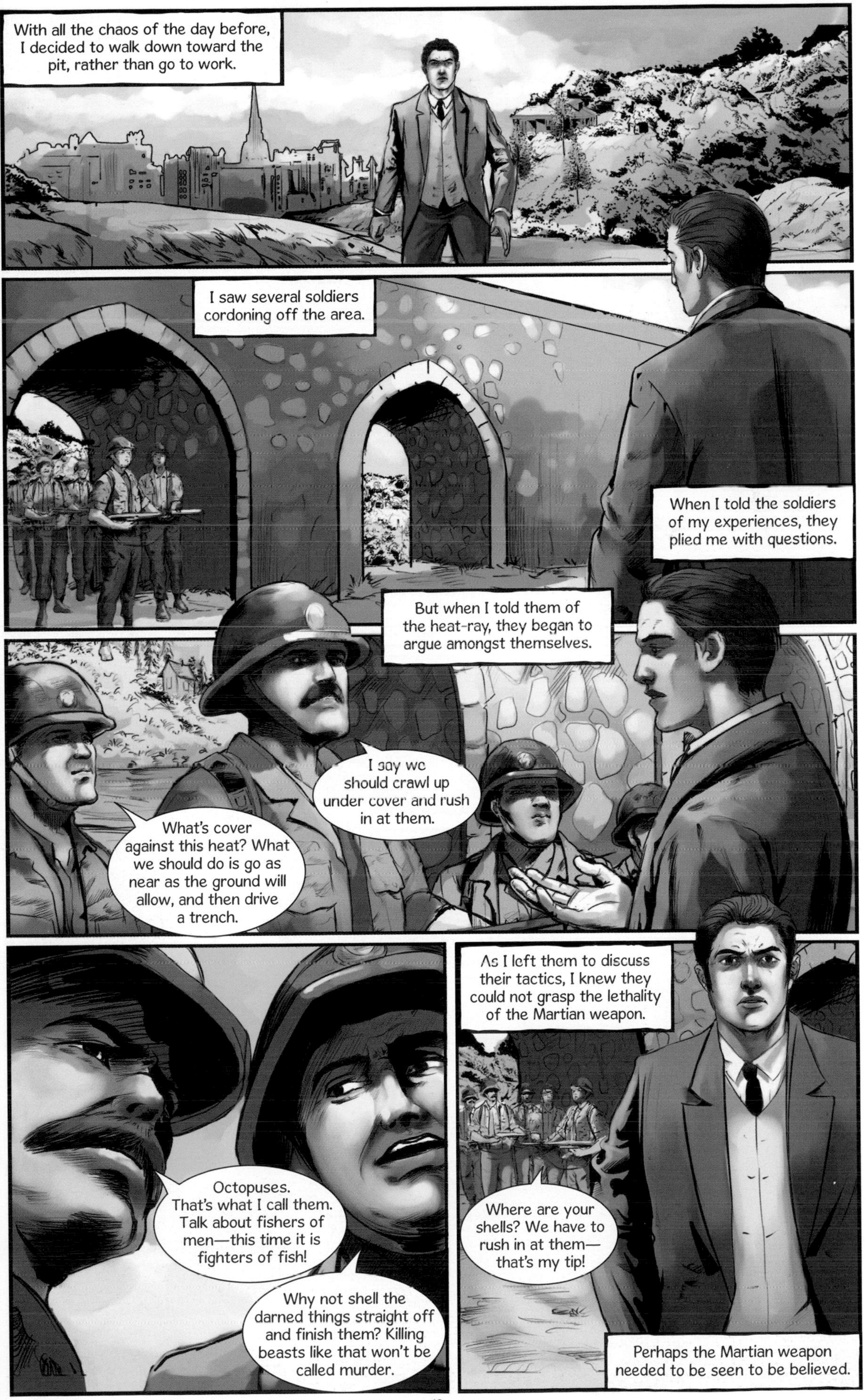

With all the chaos of the day before, I decided to walk down toward the pit, rather than go to work.
I saw several soldiers cordoning off the area.
When I told the soldiers of my experiences, they plied me with questions.
But when I told them of the heat-ray, they began to argue amongst themselves.
I say we should crawl up under cover and rush in at them.
What's cover against this heat? What we should do is go as near as the ground will allow, and then drive a trench.
Octopuses. That's what I call them. Talk about fishers of men—this time it is fighters of fish!
Why not shell the darned things straight off and finish them? Killing beasts like that won't be called murder.
As I left them to discuss their tactics, I knew they could not grasp the lethality of the Martian weapon.
Where are your shells? We have to rush in at them—that's my tip!
Perhaps the Martian weapon needed to be seen to be believed.

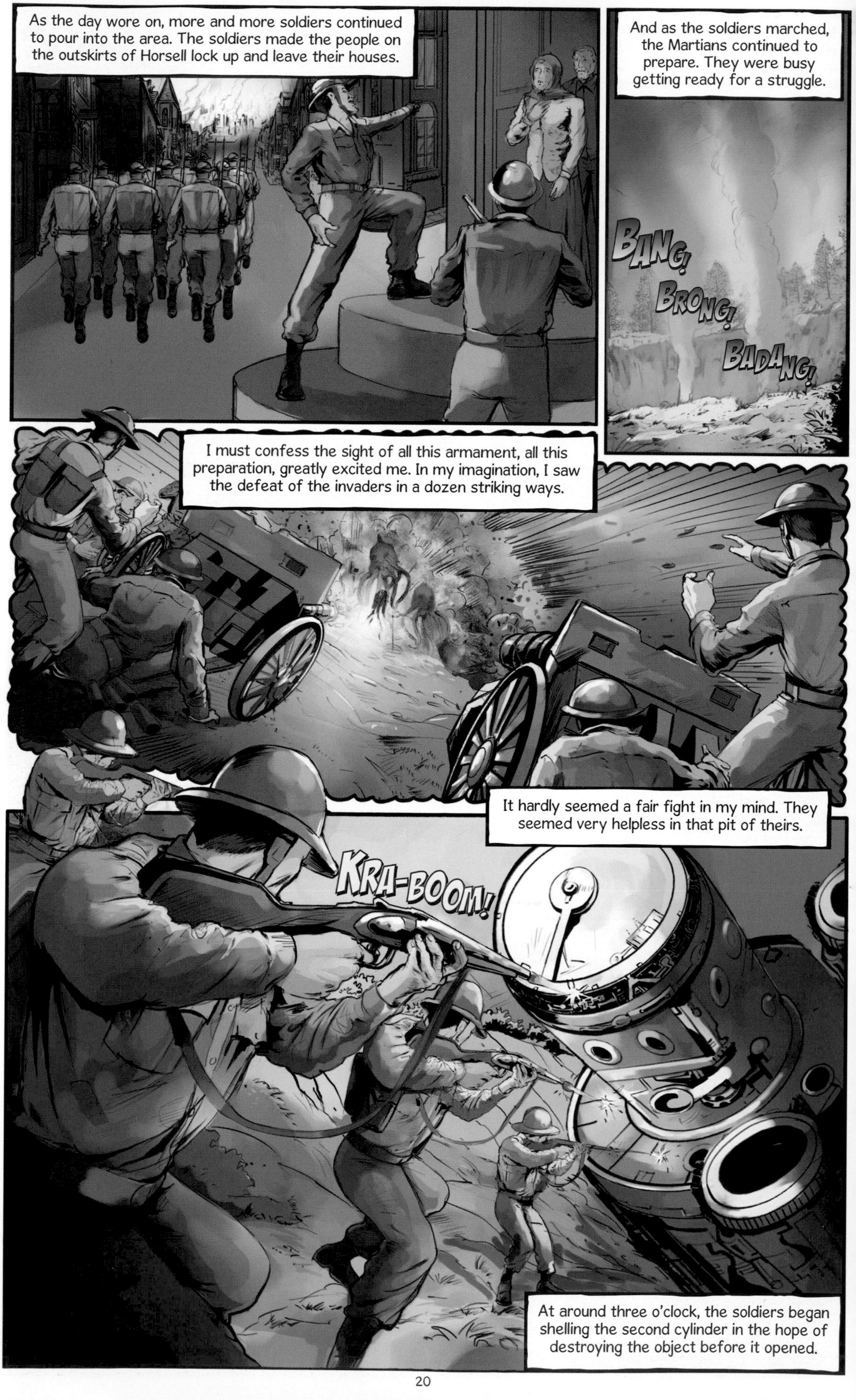
As the day wore on, more and more soldiers continued to pour into the area. The soldiers made the people on the outskirts of Horsell lock up and leave their houses.
And as the soldiers marched, the Martians continued to prepare. They were busy getting ready for a struggle.
BANG!
BRONG!
BADANG!
I must confess the sight of all this armament, all this preparation, greatly excited me. In my imagination, I saw the defeat of the invaders in a dozen striking ways.
It hardly seemed a fair fight in my mind. They seemed very helpless in that pit of theirs.
KRA-BOOM!
At around three o'clock, the soldiers began shelling the second cylinder in the hope of destroying the object before it opened.

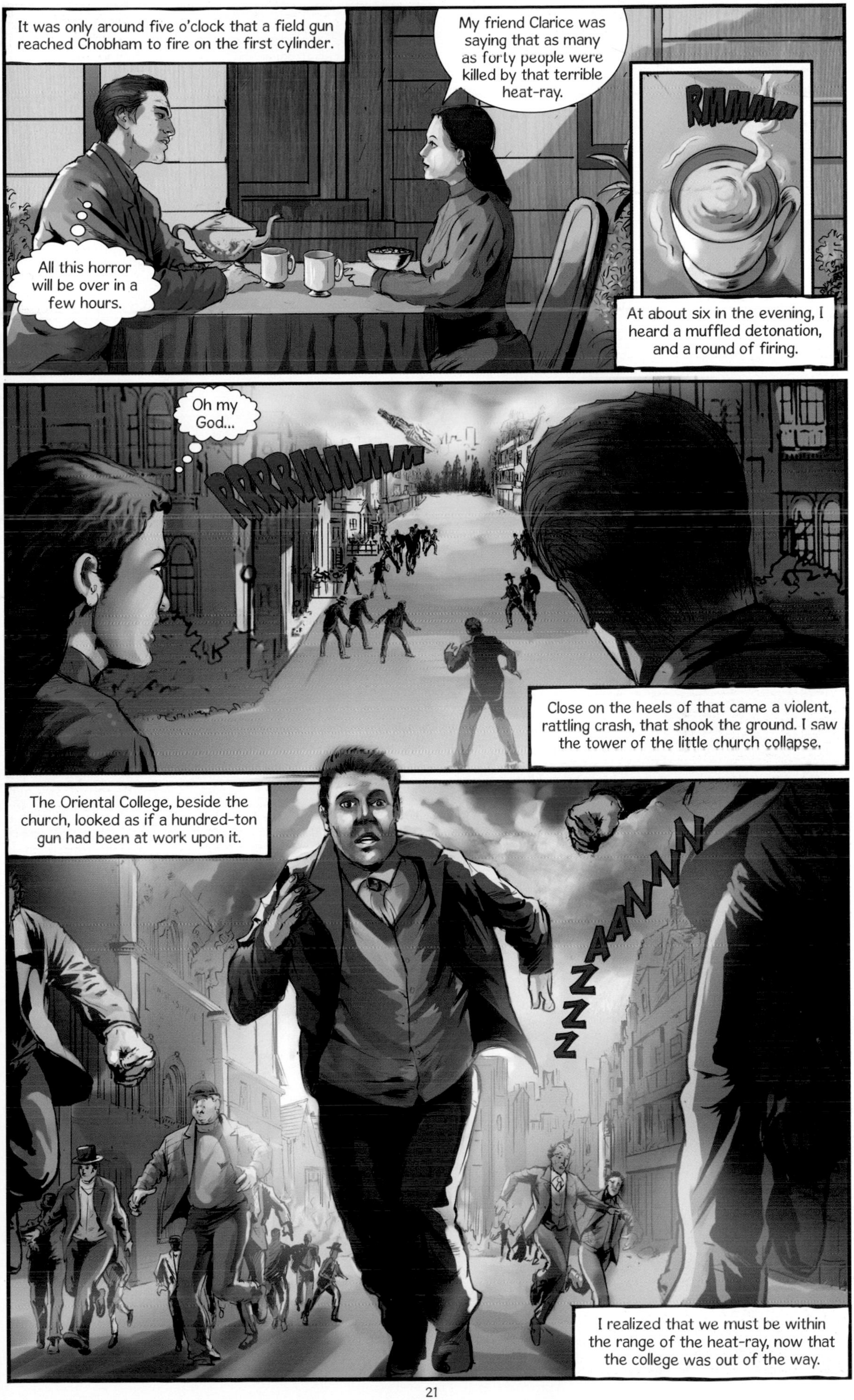
It was only around five o'clock that a field gun reached Chobham to fire on the first cylinder.
My friend Clarice was saying that as many as forty people were killed by that terrible heat-ray.
All this horror will be over in a few hours.
At about six in the evening, I heard a muffled detonation, and a round of firing.
Oh my God...
Close on the heels of that came a violent, rattling crash, that shook the ground. I saw the tower of the little church collapse.
The Oriental College, beside the church, looked as if a hundred-ton gun had been at work upon it.
I realized that we must be within the range of the heat-ray, now that the college was out of the way.

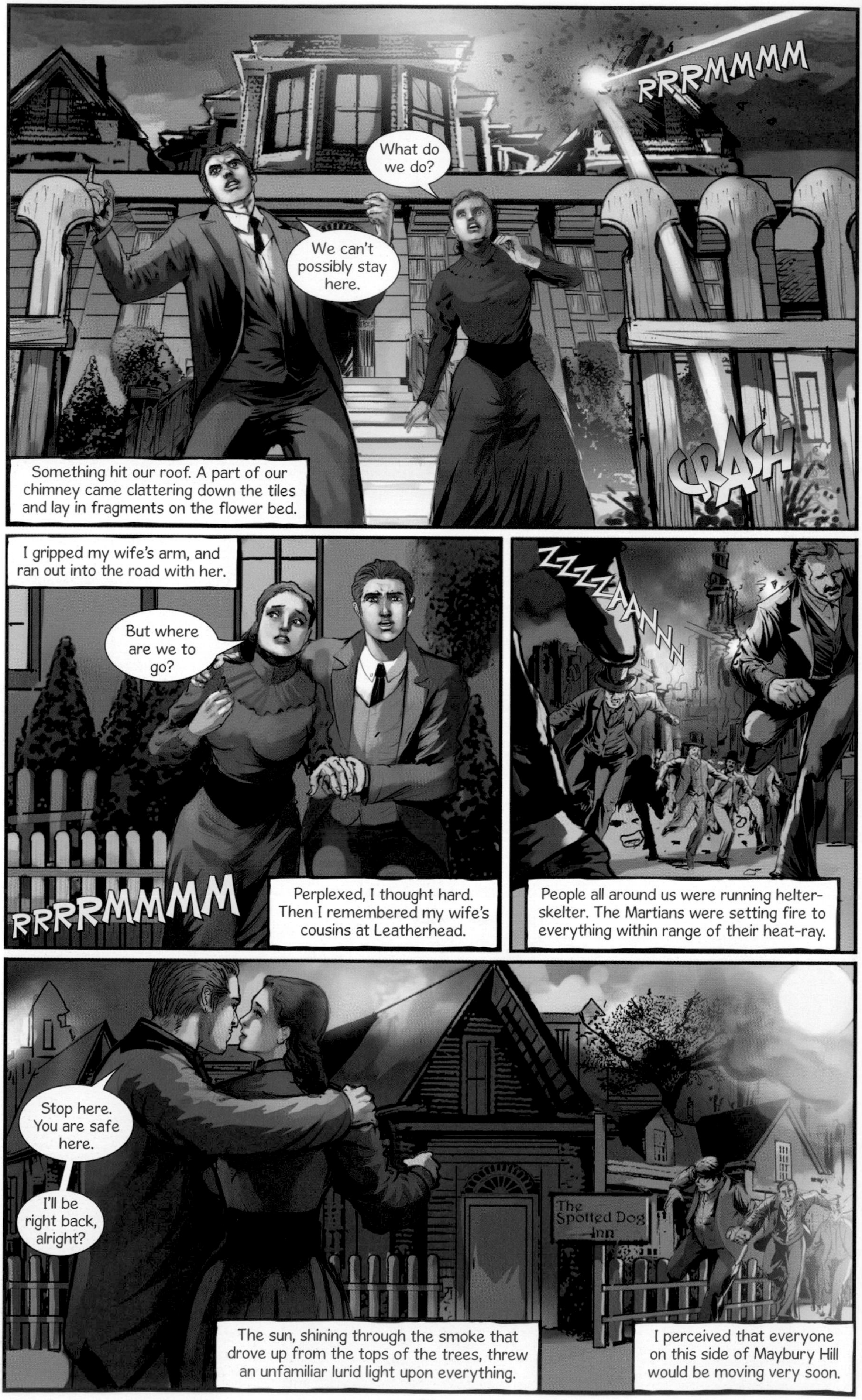
RRRMMMM
What do we do?
We can't possibly stay here.
Something hit our roof. A part of our chimney came clattering down the tiles and lay in fragments on the flower bed.
CRASH
I gripped my wife's arm, and ran out into the road with her.
But where are we to go?
RRRRMMMM
Perplexed, I thought hard. Then I remembered my wife's cousins at Leatherhead.
ZZZZAANNN
People all around us were running helter-skelter. The Martians were setting fire to everything within range of their heat-ray.
Stop here. You are safe here.
I'll be right back, alright?
The Spotted Dog Inn
The sun, shining through the smoke that drove up from the tops of the trees, threw an unfamiliar lurid light upon everything.
I perceived that everyone on this side of Maybury Hill would be moving very soon.

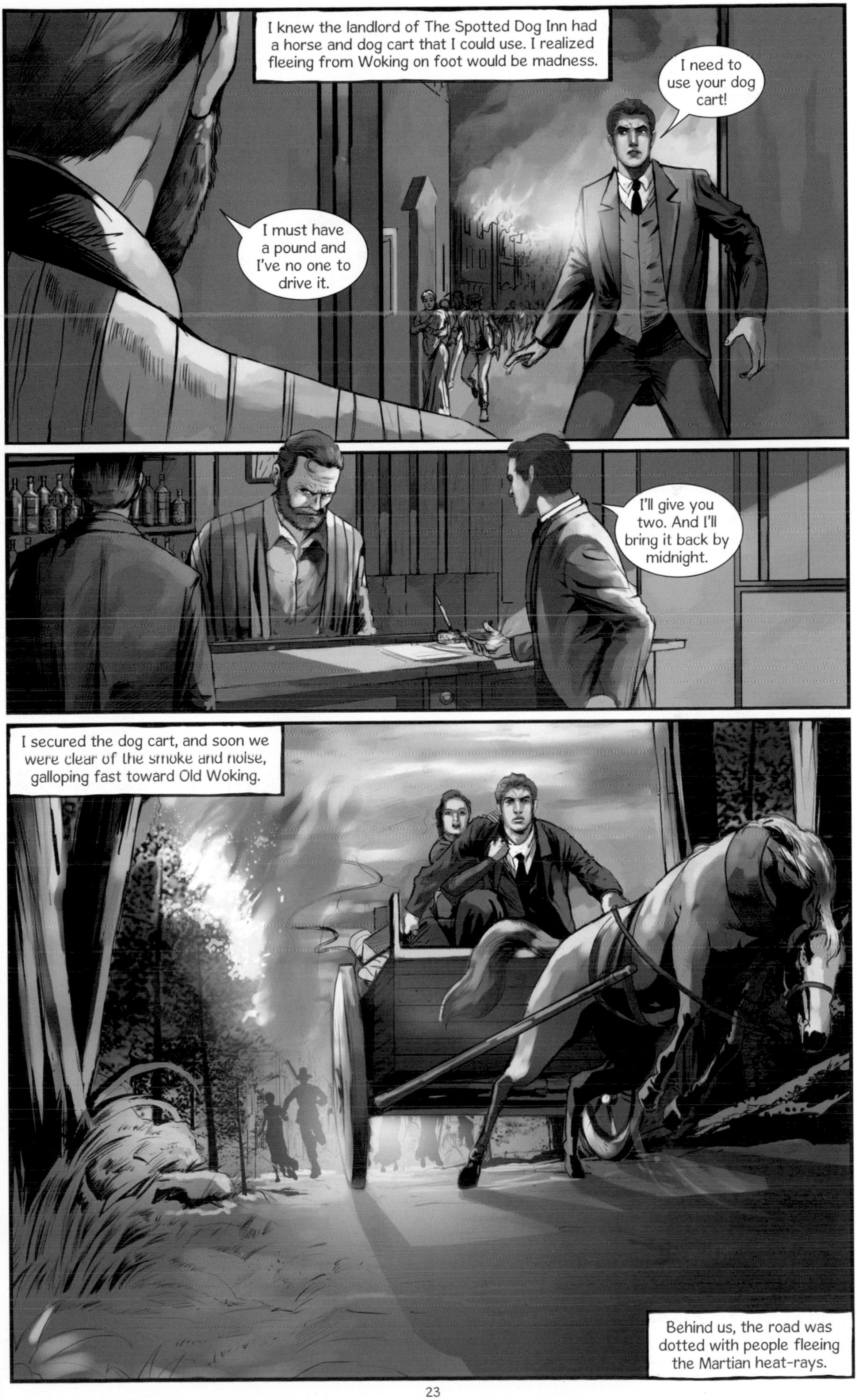
I knew the landlord of The Spotted Dog Inn had a horse and dog cart that I could use. I realized fleeing from Woking on foot would be madness.
I need to use your dog cart!
I must have a pound and I've no one to drive it.
I'll give you two. And I'll bring it back by midnight.
I secured the dog cart, and soon we were clear of the smoke and noise, galloping fast toward Old Woking.
Behind us, the road was dotted with people fleeing the Martian heat-rays.

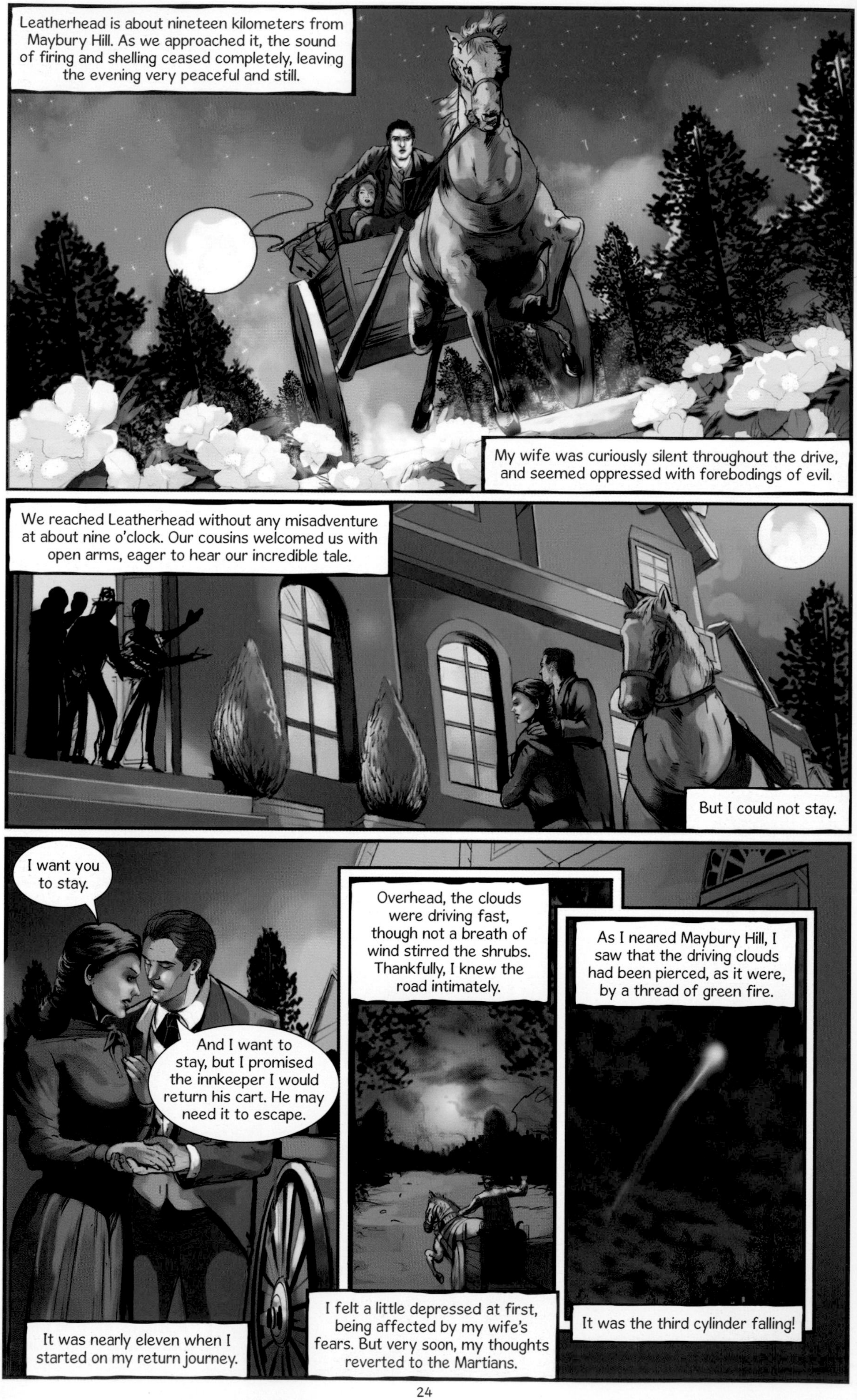

Leatherhead is about nineteen kilometers from Maybury Hill. As we approached it, the sound of firing and shelling ceased completely, leaving the evening very peaceful and still.
My wife was curiously silent throughout the drive, and seemed oppressed with forebodings of evil.
We reached Leatherhead without any misadventure at about nine o'clock. Our cousins welcomed us with open arms, eager to hear our incredible tale.
But I could not stay.
I want you to stay.
And I want to stay, but I promised the innkeeper I would return his cart. He may need it to escape.
It was nearly eleven when I started on my return journey.
Overhead, the clouds were driving fast, though not a breath of wind stirred the shrubs. Thankfully, I knew the road intimately.
I felt a little depressed at first, being affected by my wife's fears. But very soon, my thoughts reverted to the Martians.
As I neared Maybury Hill, I saw that the driving clouds had been pierced, as it were, by a thread of green fire.
It was the third cylinder falling!

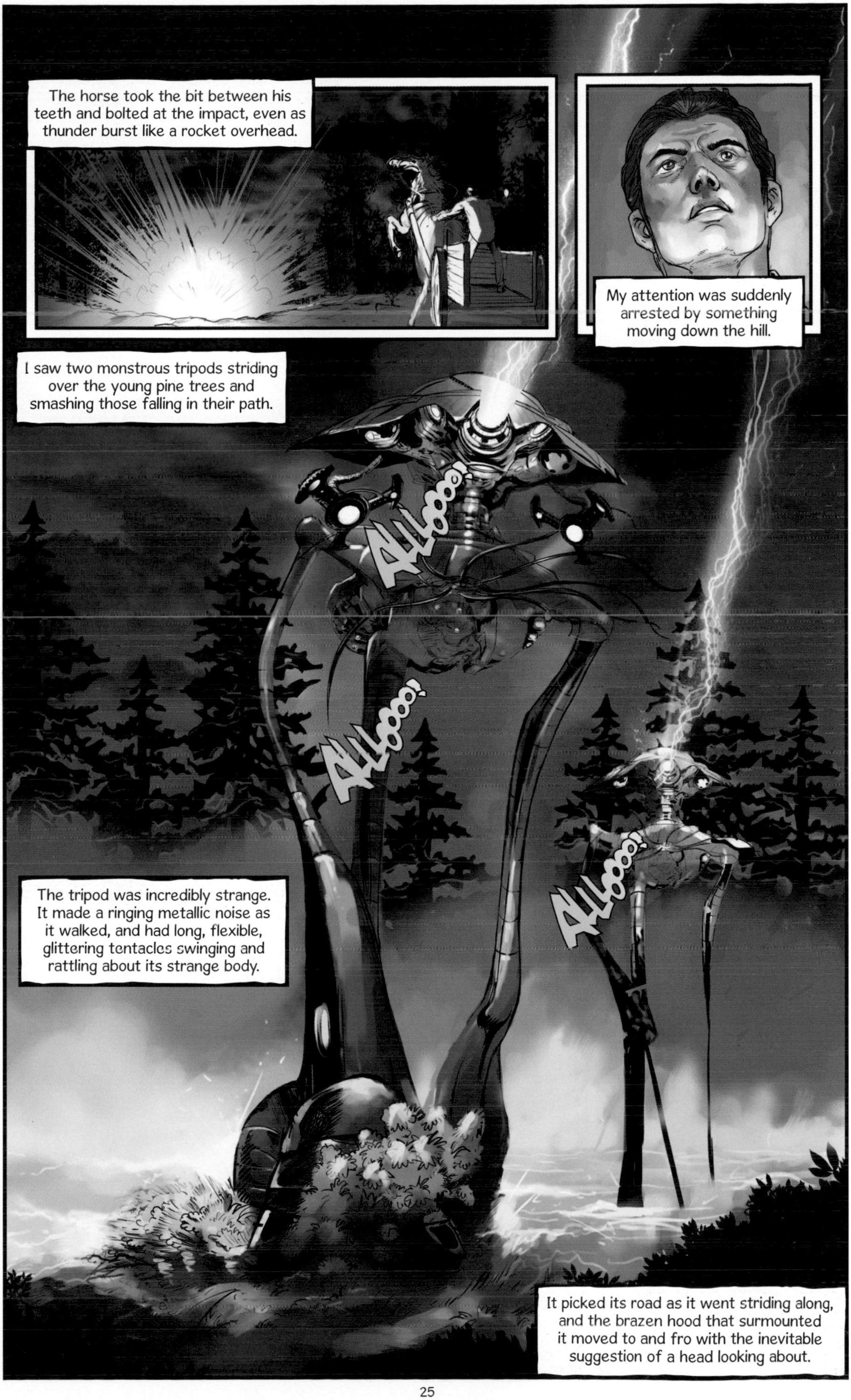
The horse took the bit between his teeth and bolted at the impact, even as thunder burst like a rocket overhead.
My attention was suddenly arrested by something moving down the hill.
I saw two monstrous tripods striding over the young pine trees and smashing those falling in their path.
ALLOOOO!
ALLOOOO!
ALLOOOO!
The tripod was incredibly strange. It made a ringing metallic noise as it walked, and had long, flexible, glittering tentacles swinging and rattling about its strange body.
It picked its road as it went striding along, and the brazen hood that surmounted it moved to and fro with the inevitable suggestion of a head looking about.

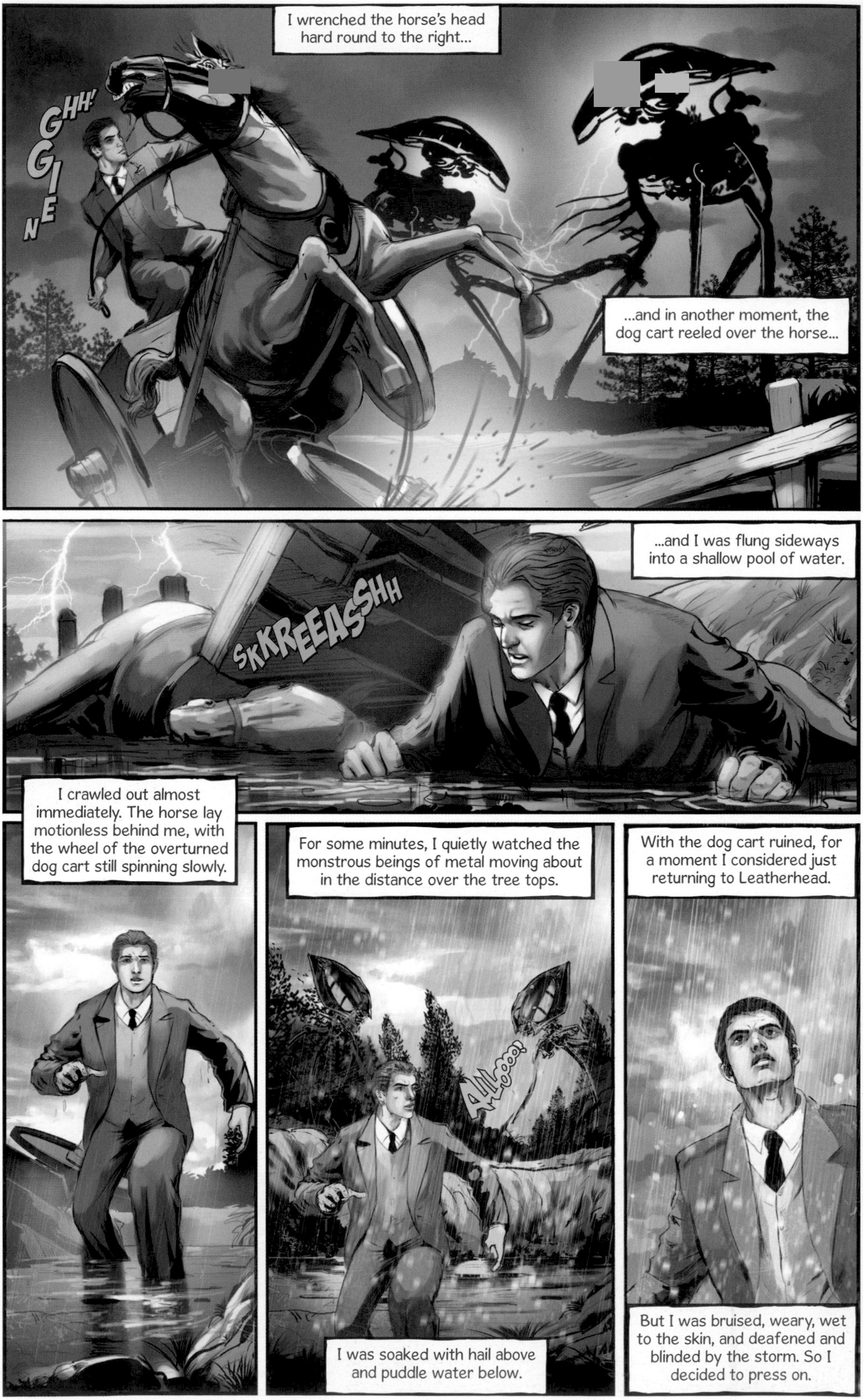
I wrenched the horse's head hard round to the right...
NEIGGHH!
...and in another moment, the dog cart reeled over the horse...
...and I was flung sideways into a shallow pool of water.
SKKREEASSHH
I crawled out almost immediately. The horse lay motionless behind me, with the wheel of the overturned dog cart still spinning slowly.
For some minutes, I quietly watched the monstrous beings of metal moving about in the distance over the tree tops.
ALLoooo!
I was soaked with hail above and puddle water below.
With the dog cart ruined, for a moment I considered just returning to Leatherhead.
But I was bruised, weary, wet to the skin, and deafened and blinded by the storm. So I decided to press on.

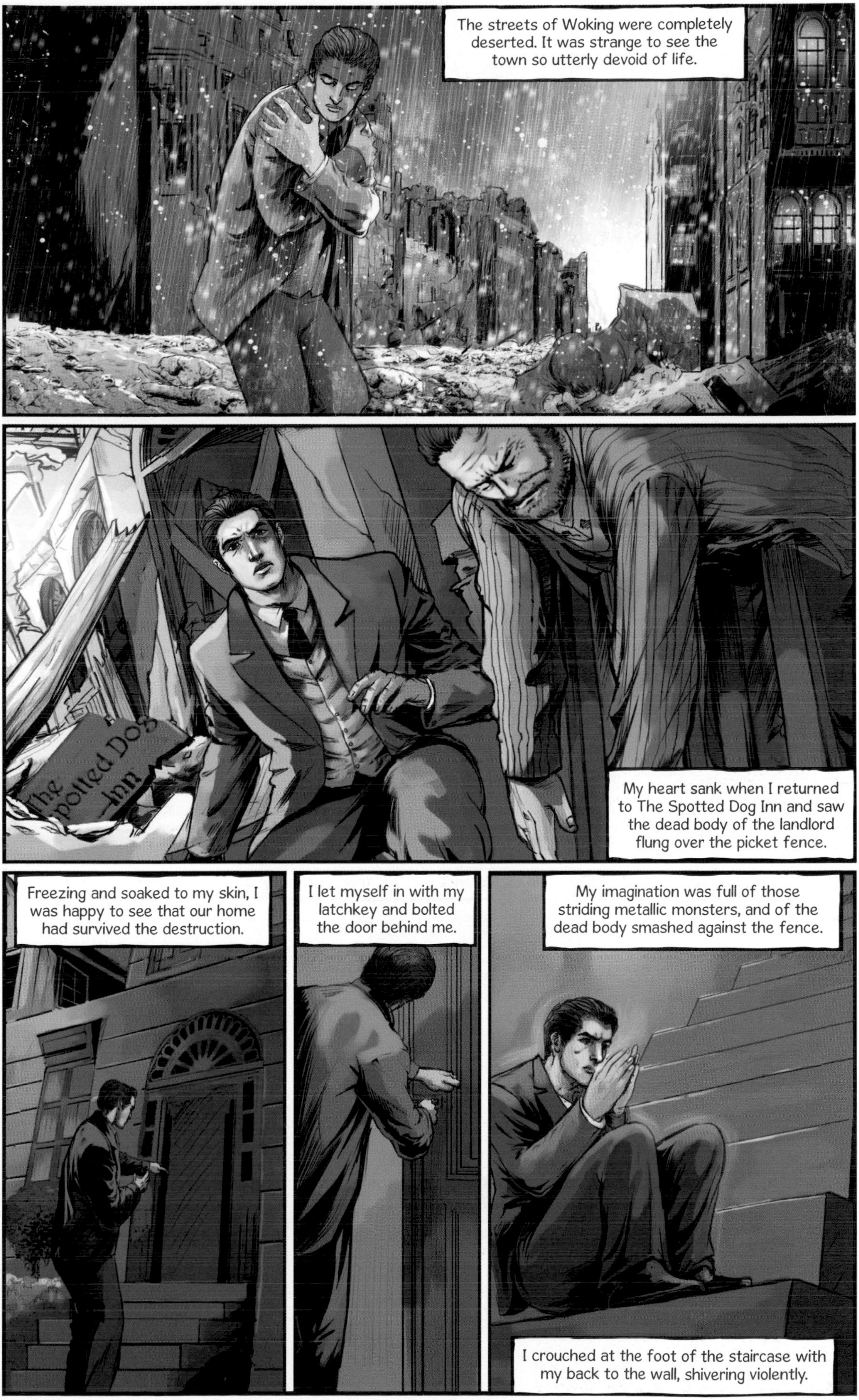
The streets of Woking were completely deserted. It was strange to see the town so utterly devoid of life.
The Spotted Dog Inn
My heart sank when I returned to The Spotted Dog Inn and saw the dead body of the landlord flung over the picket fence.
Freezing and soaked to my skin, I was happy to see that our home had survived the destruction.
I let myself in with my latchkey and bolted the door behind me.
My imagination was full of those striding metallic monsters, and of the dead body smashed against the fence.
I crouched at the foot of the staircase with my back to the wall, shivering violently.

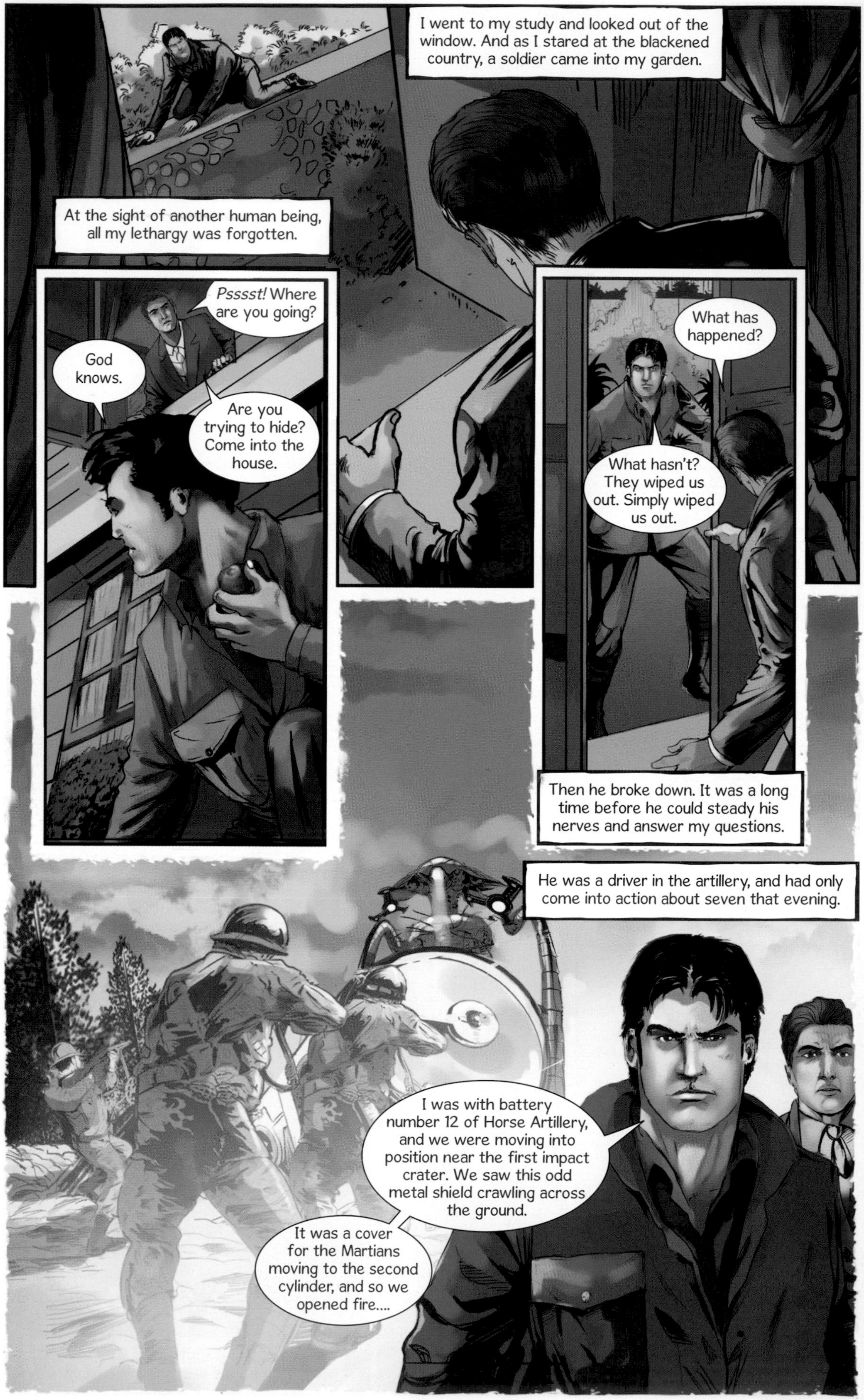
I went to my study and looked out of the window. And as I stared at the blackened country, a soldier came into my garden.
At the sight of another human being, all my lethargy was forgotten.
Psssst! Where are you going?
God knows.
Are you trying to hide? Come into the house.
What has happened?
What hasn't? They wiped us out. Simply wiped us out.
Then he broke down. It was a long time before he could steady his nerves and answer my questions.
He was a driver in the artillery, and had only come into action about seven that evening.
I was with battery number 12 of Horse Artillery, and we were moving into position near the first impact crater. We saw this odd metal shield crawling across the ground.
It was a cover for the Martians moving to the second cylinder, and so we opened fire....

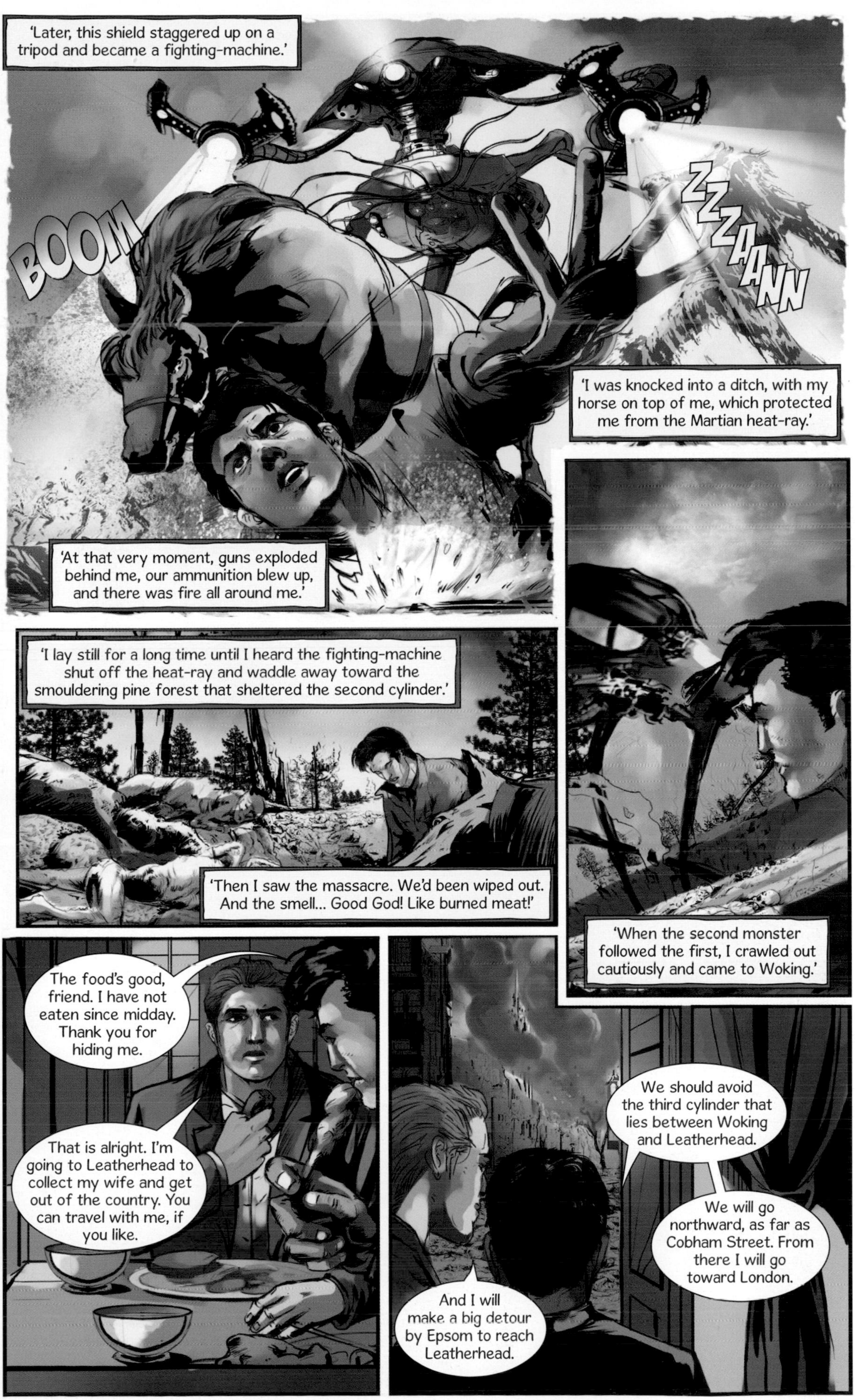
'Later, this shield staggered up on a tripod and became a fighting-machine.'
BOOM
ZZZAANN
'I was knocked into a ditch, with my horse on top of me, which protected me from the Martian heat-ray.'
'At that very moment, guns exploded behind me, our ammunition blew up, and there was fire all around me.'
'I lay still for a long time until I heard the fighting-machine shut off the heat-ray and waddle away toward the smouldering pine forest that sheltered the second cylinder.'
'Then I saw the massacre. We'd been wiped out. And the smell... Good God! Like burned meat!'
'When the second monster followed the first, I crawled out cautiously and came to Woking.'
The food's good, friend. I have not eaten since midday. Thank you for hiding me.
That is alright. I'm going to Leatherhead to collect my wife and get out of the country. You can travel with me, if you like.
We should avoid the third cylinder that lies between Woking and Leatherhead.
We will go northward, as far as Cobham Street. From there I will go toward London.
And I will make a big detour by Epsom to reach Leatherhead.

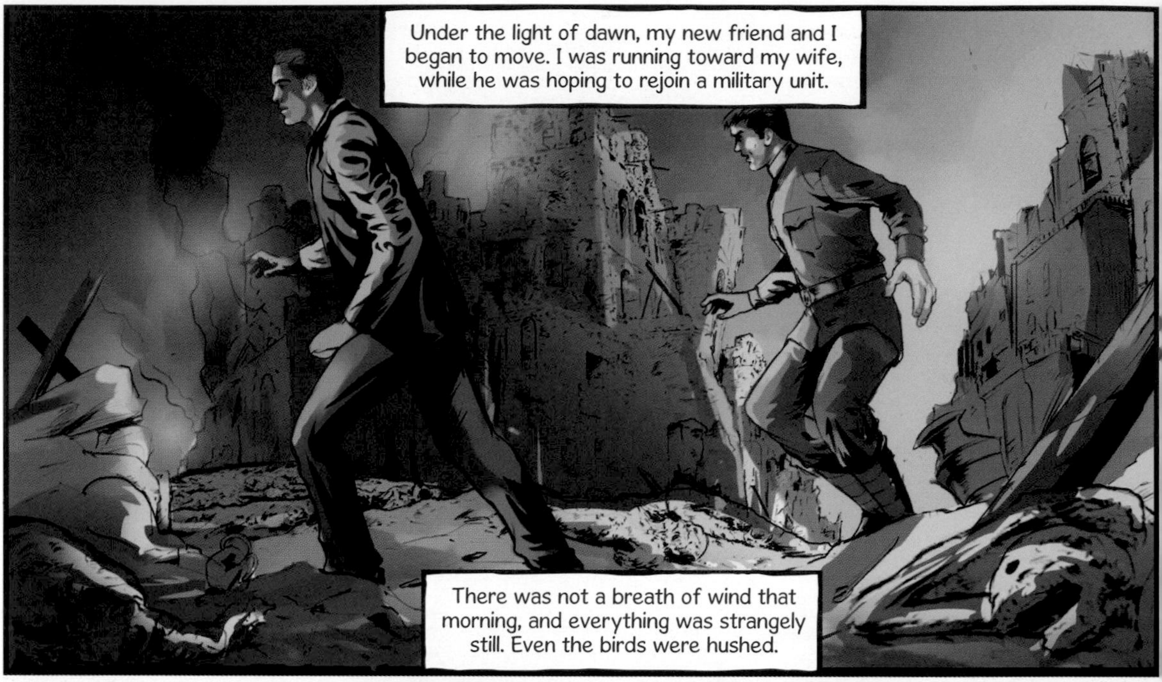
Under the light of dawn, my new friend and I began to move. I was running toward my wife, while he was hoping to rejoin a military unit.
There was not a breath of wind that morning, and everything was strangely still. Even the birds were hushed.

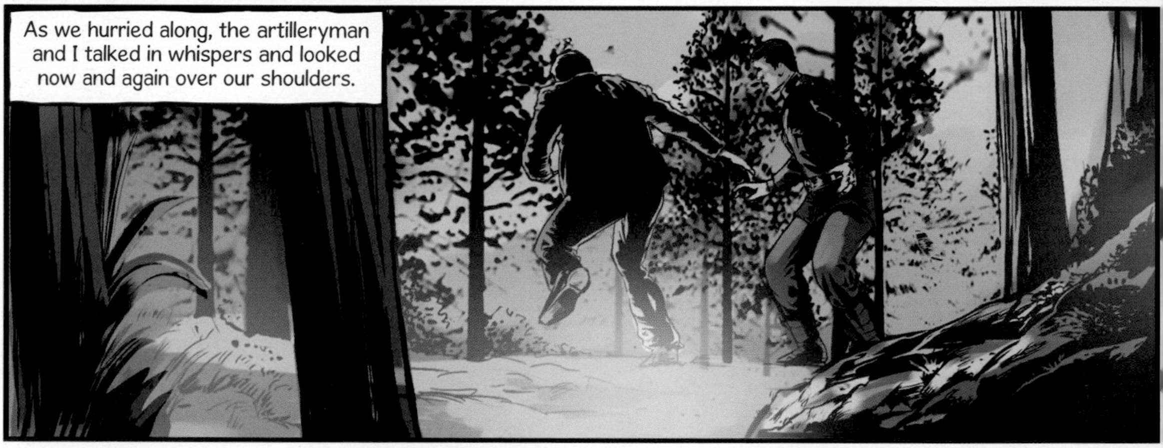
As we hurried along, the artilleryman and I talked in whispers and looked now and again over our shoulders.

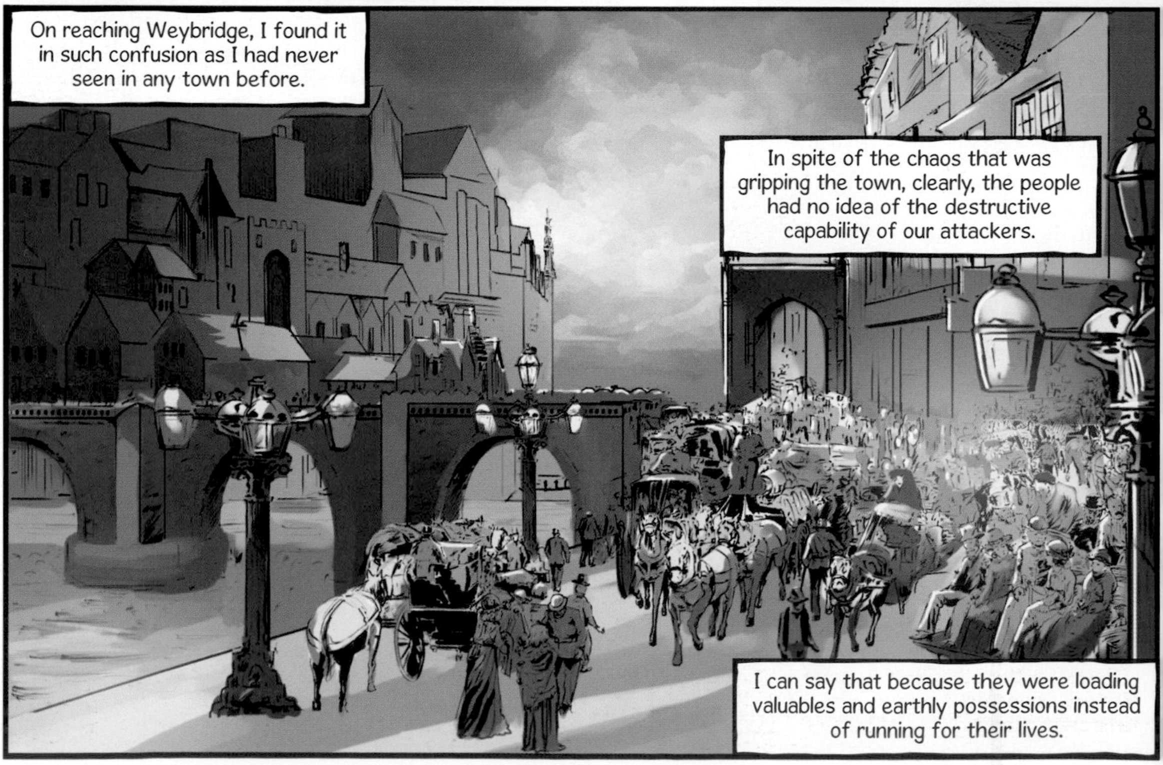
On reaching Weybridge, I found it in such confusion as I had never seen in any town before.
In spite of the chaos that was gripping the town, clearly, the people had no idea of the destructive capability of our attackers.
I can say that because they were loading valuables and earthly possessions instead of running for their lives.

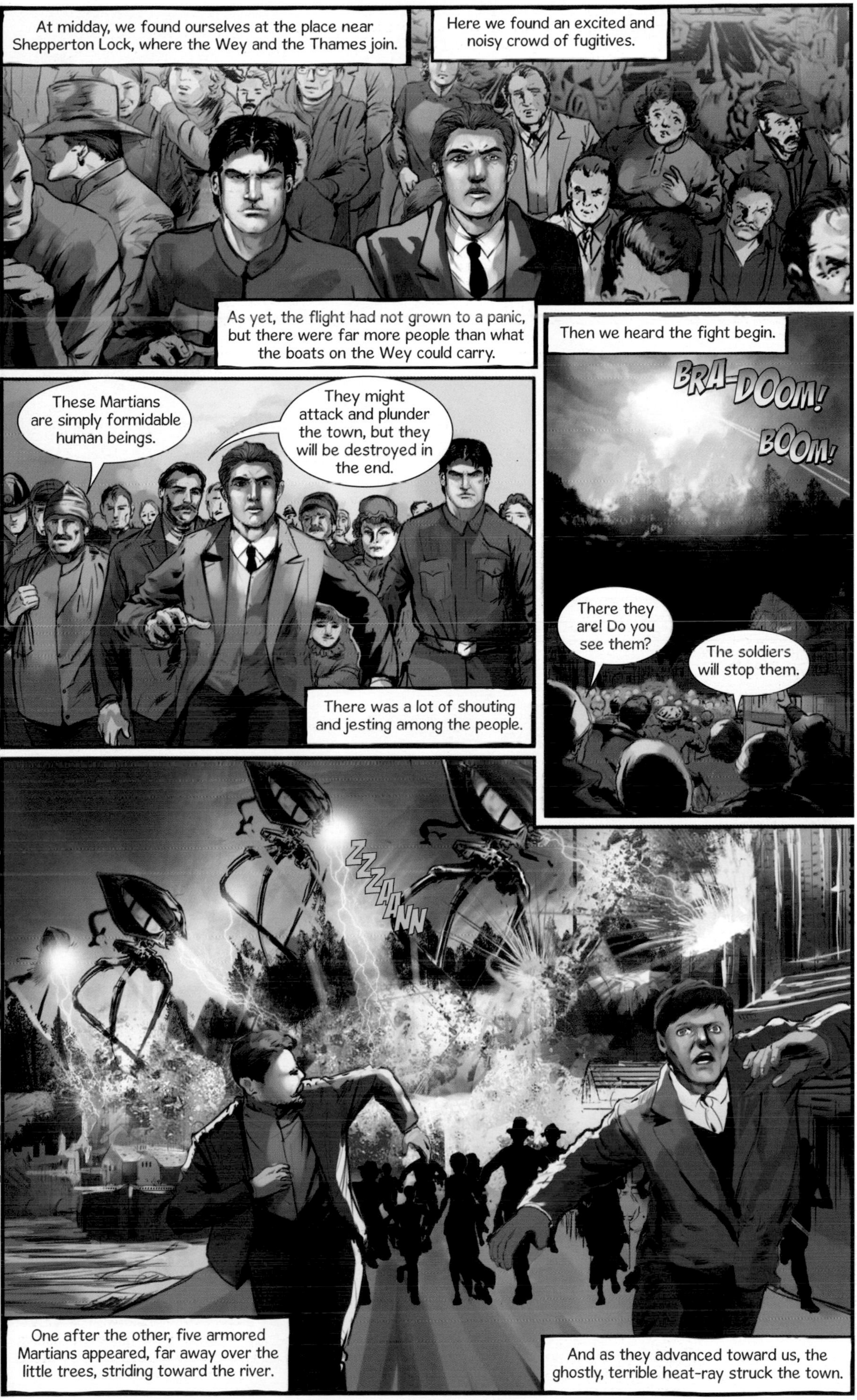

At midday, we found ourselves at the place near Shepperton Lock, where the Wey and the Thames join.
Here we found an excited and noisy crowd of fugitives.
As yet, the flight had not grown to a panic, but there were far more people than what the boats on the Wey could carry.
Then we heard the fight begin.
BRA-DOOM!
BOOM!
These Martians are simply formidable human beings.
They might attack and plunder the town, but they will be destroyed in the end.
There was a lot of shouting and jesting among the people.
There they are! Do you see them?
The soldiers will stop them.
ZZZAANN
One after the other, five armored Martians appeared, far away over the little trees, striding toward the river.
And as they advanced toward us, the ghostly, terrible heat-ray struck the town.

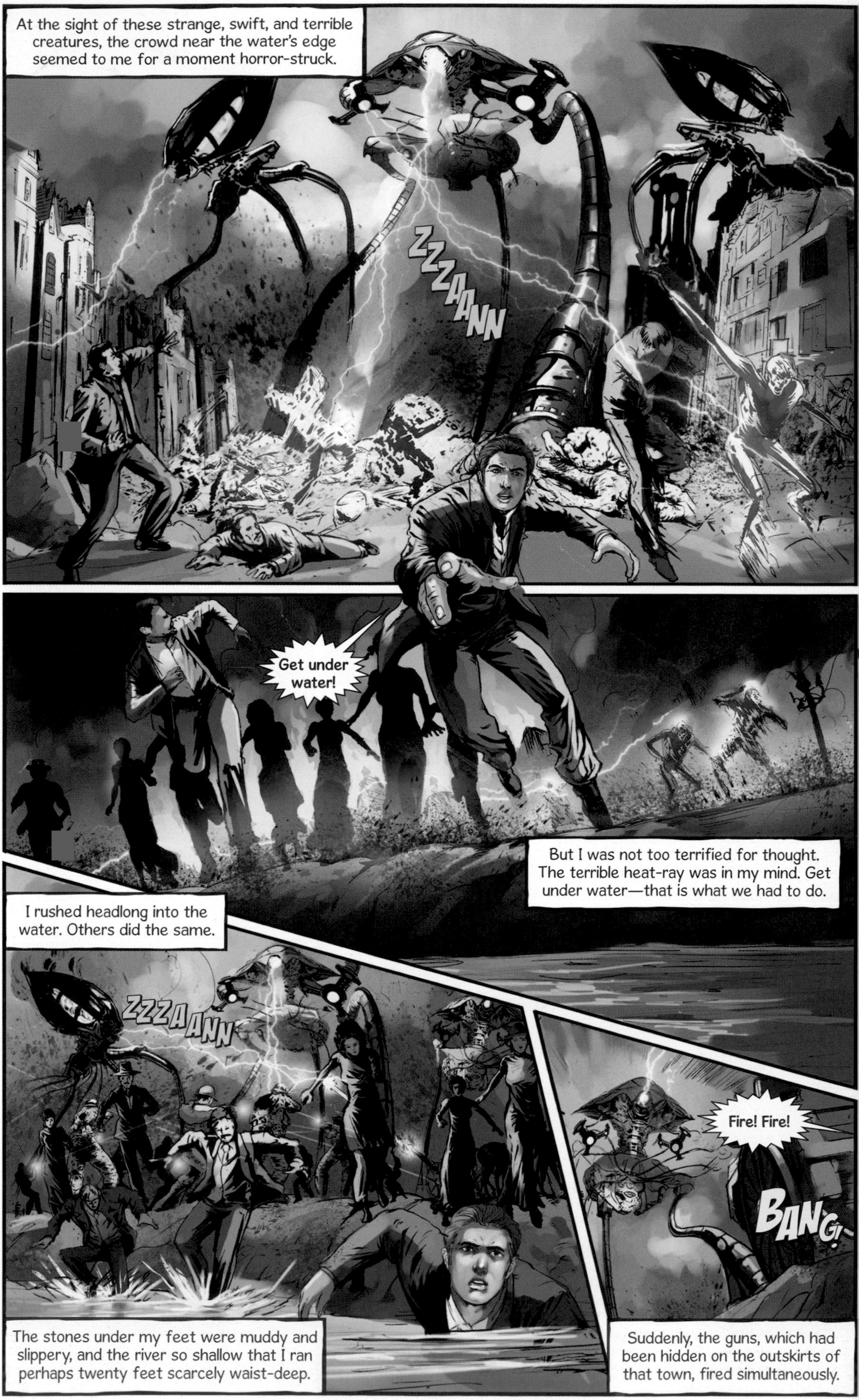
At the sight of these strange, swift, and terrible creatures, the crowd near the water's edge seemed to me for a moment horror-struck.
ZZZAANN
Get under water!
But I was not too terrified for thought. The terrible heat-ray was in my mind. Get under water—that is what we had to do.
I rushed headlong into the water. Others did the same.
ZZZAANN
The stones under my feet were muddy and slippery, and the river so shallow that I ran perhaps twenty feet scarcely waist-deep.
Fire! Fire!
BANG!
Suddenly, the guns, which had been hidden on the outskirts of that town, fired simultaneously.

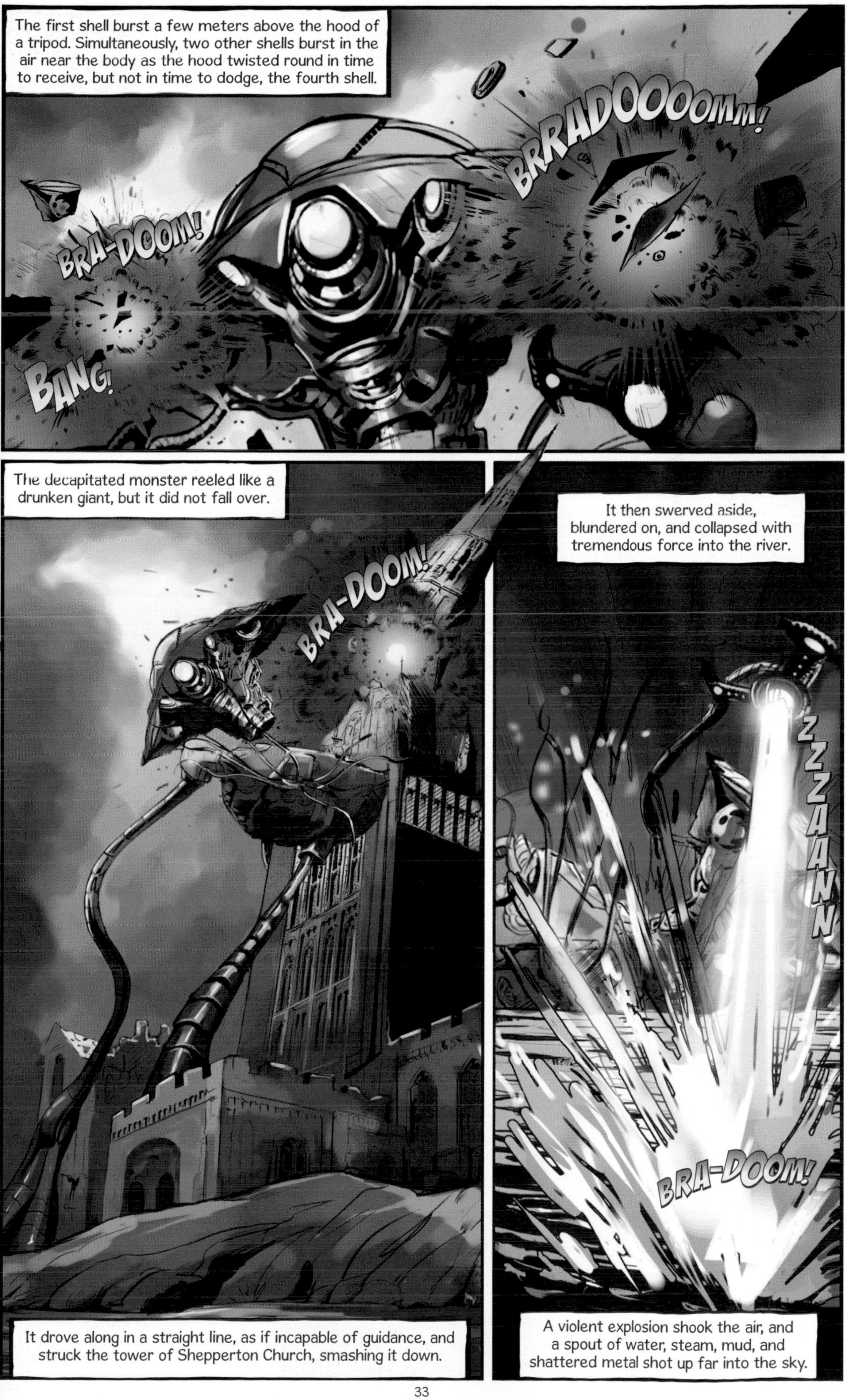
The first shell burst a few meters above the hood of a tripod. Simultaneously, two other shells burst in the air near the body as the hood twisted round in time to receive, but not in time to dodge, the fourth shell.
BRRADOOOOOMM!
BRA-DOOM!
BANG!
The decapitated monster reeled like a drunken giant, but it did not fall over.
BRA-DOOM!
It drove along in a straight line, as if incapable of guidance, and struck the tower of Shepperton Church, smashing it down.
It then swerved aside, blundered on, and collapsed with tremendous force into the river.
ZZZAAANN
BRA-DOOM!
A violent explosion shook the air, and a spout of water, steam, mud, and shattered metal shot up far into the sky.

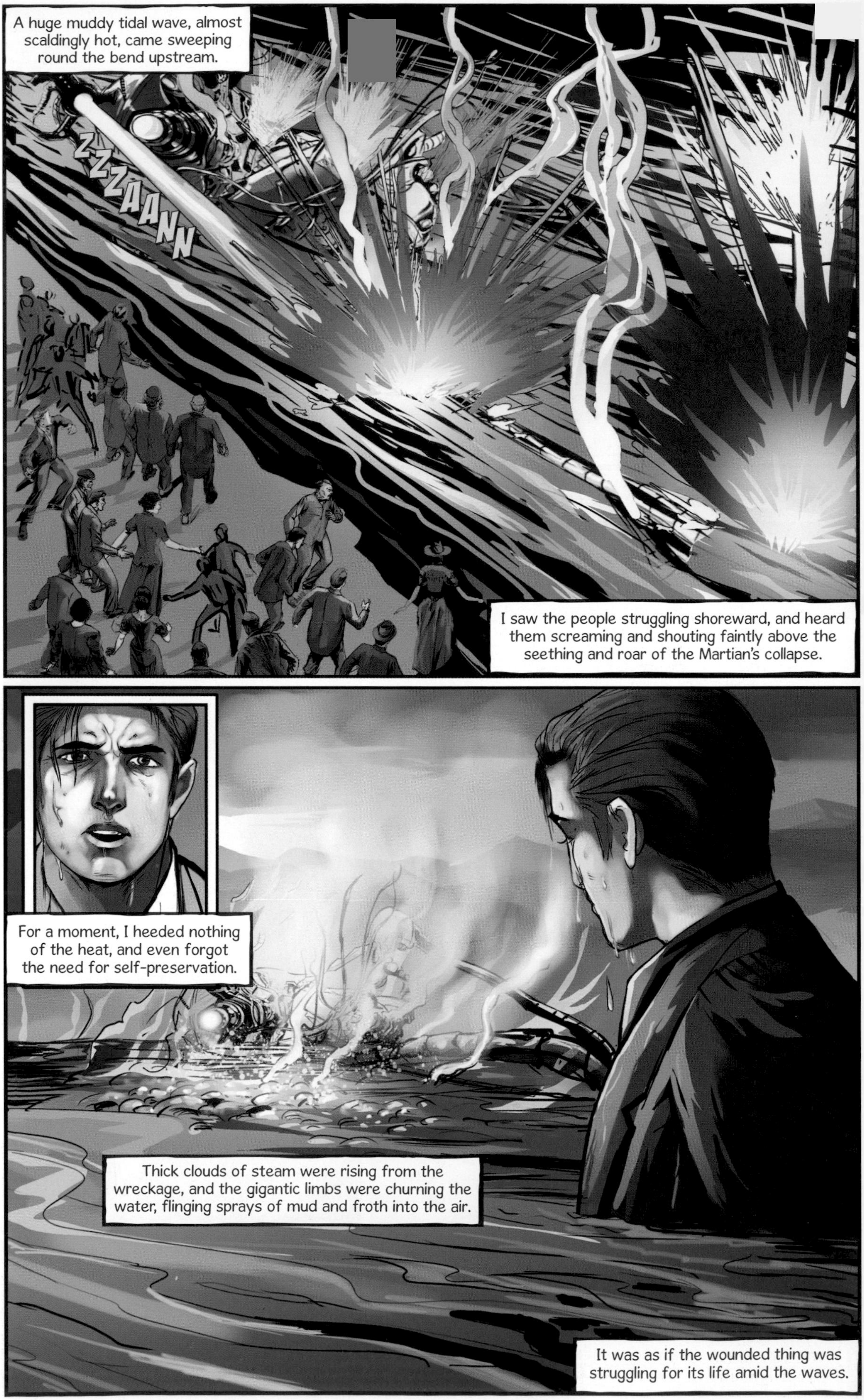

A huge muddy tidal wave, almost scaldingly hot, came sweeping round the bend upstream.
ZZZAANN
I saw the people struggling shoreward, and heard them screaming and shouting faintly above the seething and roar of the Martian's collapse.
For a moment, I heeded nothing of the heat, and even forgot the need for self-preservation.
Thick clouds of steam were rising from the wreckage, and the gigantic limbs were churning the water, flinging sprays of mud and froth into the air.
It was as if the wounded thing was struggling for its life amid the waves.

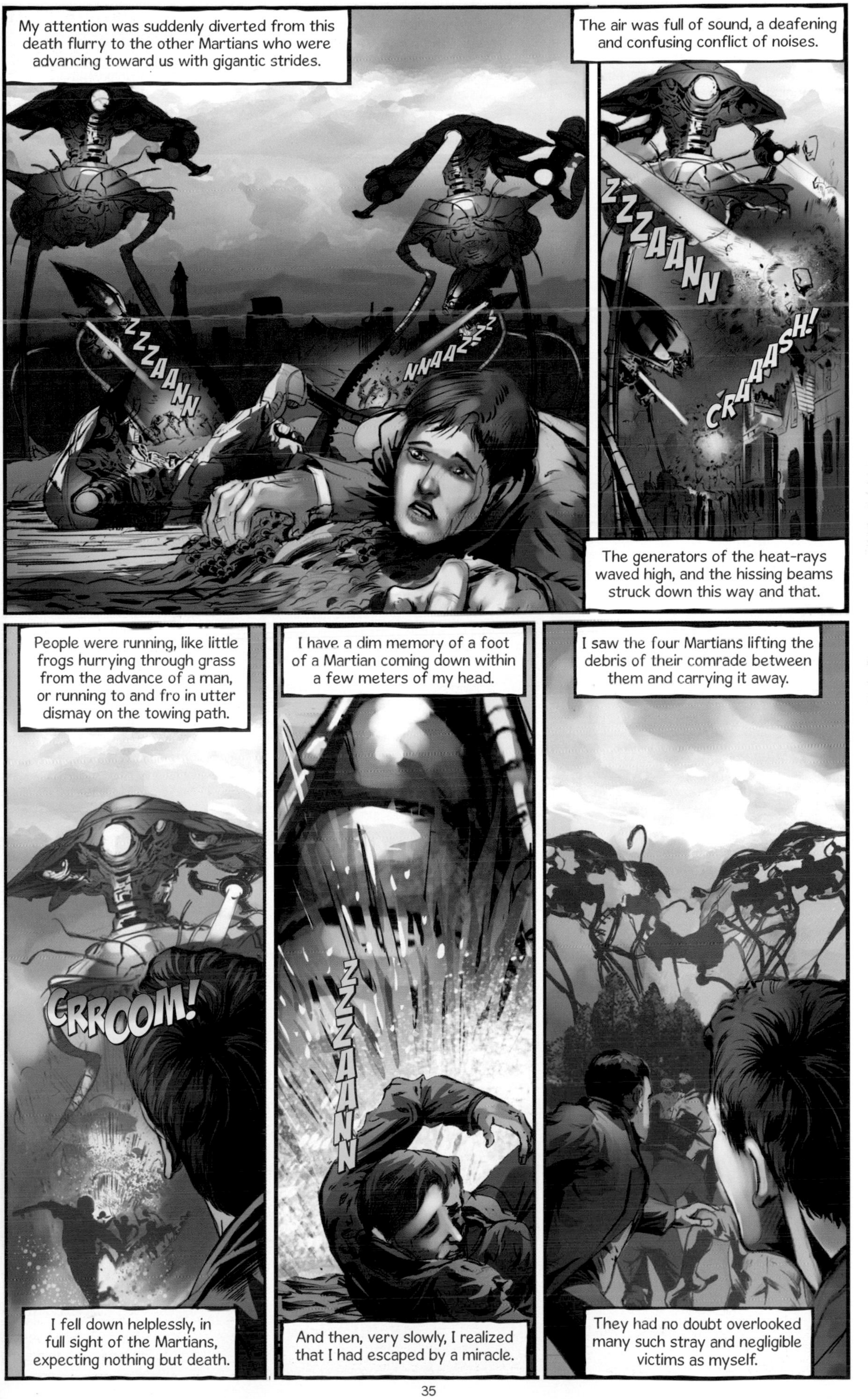
My attention was suddenly diverted from this death flurry to the other Martians who were advancing toward us with gigantic strides.
ZZZAANN
NNAAZZZ
The air was full of sound, a deafening and confusing conflict of noises.
ZZZAANN
CRAAASH!
The generators of the heat-rays waved high, and the hissing beams struck down this way and that.
People were running, like little frogs hurrying through grass from the advance of a man, or running to and fro in utter dismay on the towing path.
CRROOM!
I fell down helplessly, in full sight of the Martians, expecting nothing but death.
I have a dim memory of a foot of a Martian coming down within a few meters of my head.
ZZZAANN
And then, very slowly, I realized that I had escaped by a miracle.
I saw the four Martians lifting the debris of their comrade between them and carrying it away.
They had no doubt overlooked many such stray and negligible victims as myself.

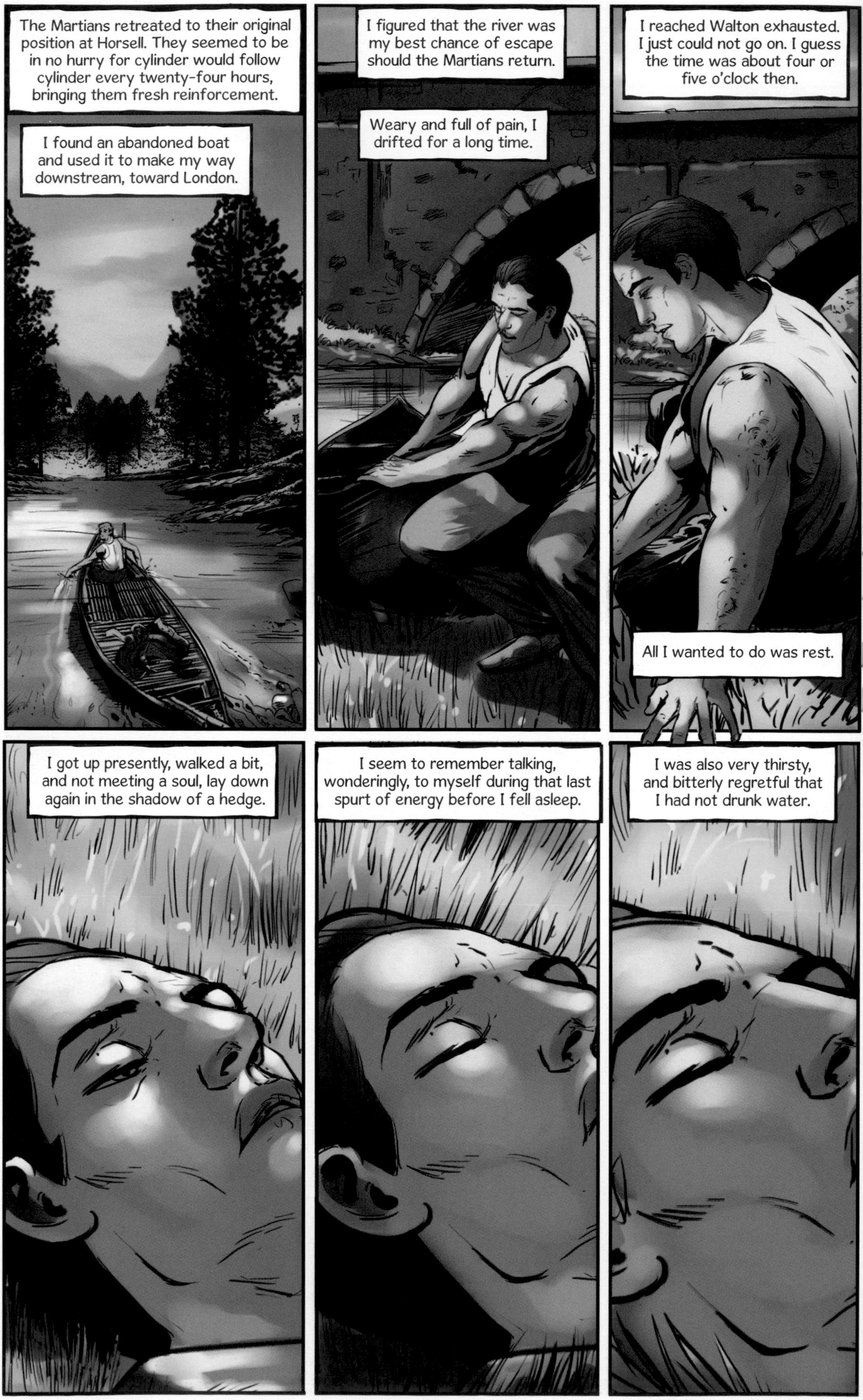
The Martians retreated to their original position at Horsell. They seemed to be in no hurry for cylinder would follow cylinder every twenty-four hours, bringing them fresh reinforcement.
I found an abandoned boat and used it to make my way downstream, toward London.
I figured that the river was my best chance of escape should the Martians return.
Weary and full of pain, I drifted for a long time.
I reached Walton exhausted. I just could not go on. I guess the time was about four or five o'clock then.
All I wanted to do was rest.
I got up presently, walked a bit, and not meeting a soul, lay down again in the shadow of a hedge.
I seem to remember talking, wonderingly, to myself during that last spurt of energy before I fell asleep.
I was also very thirsty, and bitterly regretful that I had not drunk water.

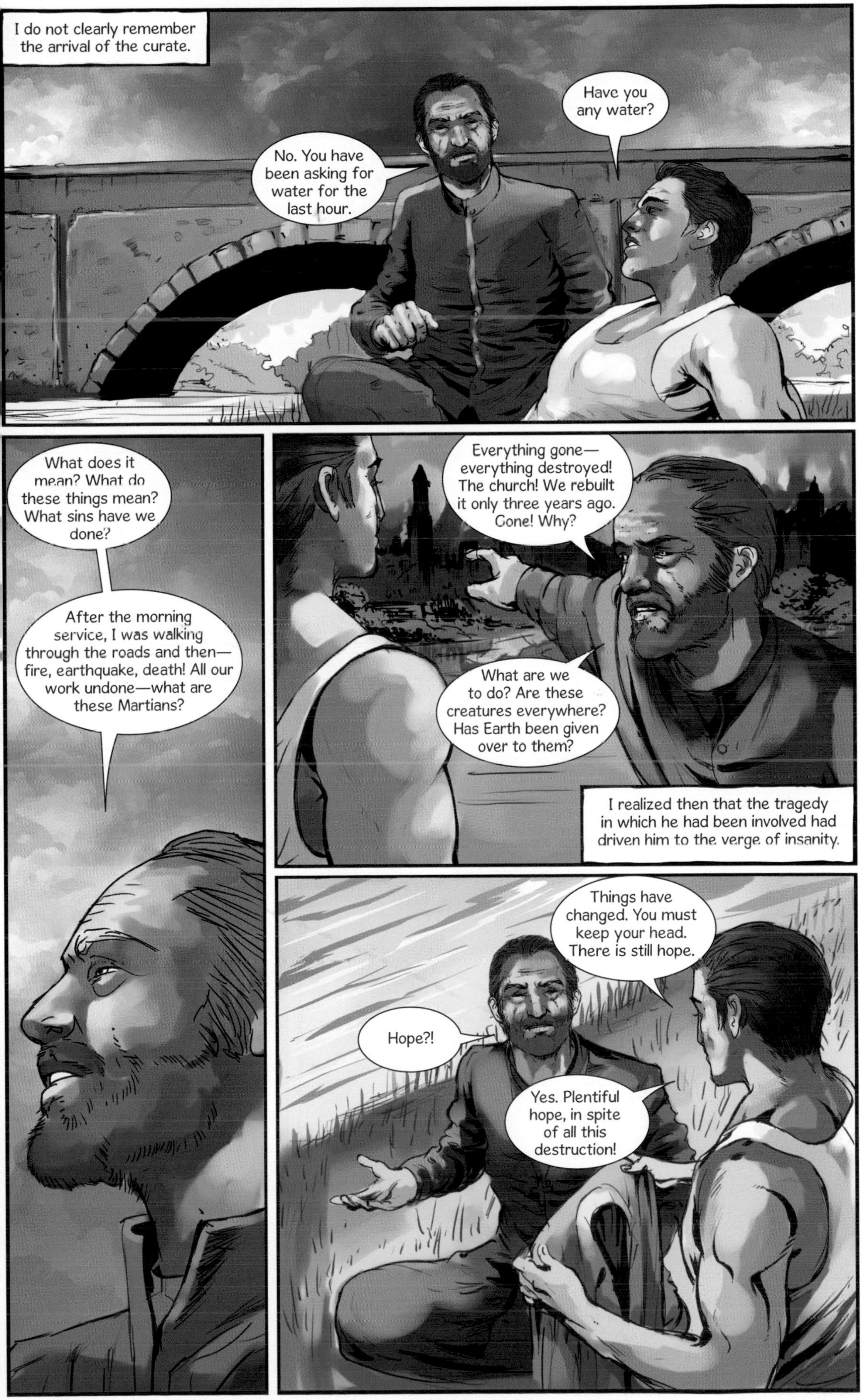
I do not clearly remember the arrival of the curate.
Have you any water?
No. You have been asking for water for the last hour.
What does it mean? What do these things mean? What sins have we done?
After the morning service, I was walking through the roads and then—fire, earthquake, death! All our work undone—what are these Martians?
Everything gone—everything destroyed! The church! We rebuilt it only three years ago. Gone! Why?
What are we to do? Are these creatures everywhere? Has Earth been given over to them?
I realized then that the tragedy in which he had been involved had driven him to the verge of insanity.
Things have changed. You must keep your head. There is still hope.
Hope?!
Yes. Plentiful hope, in spite of all this destruction!

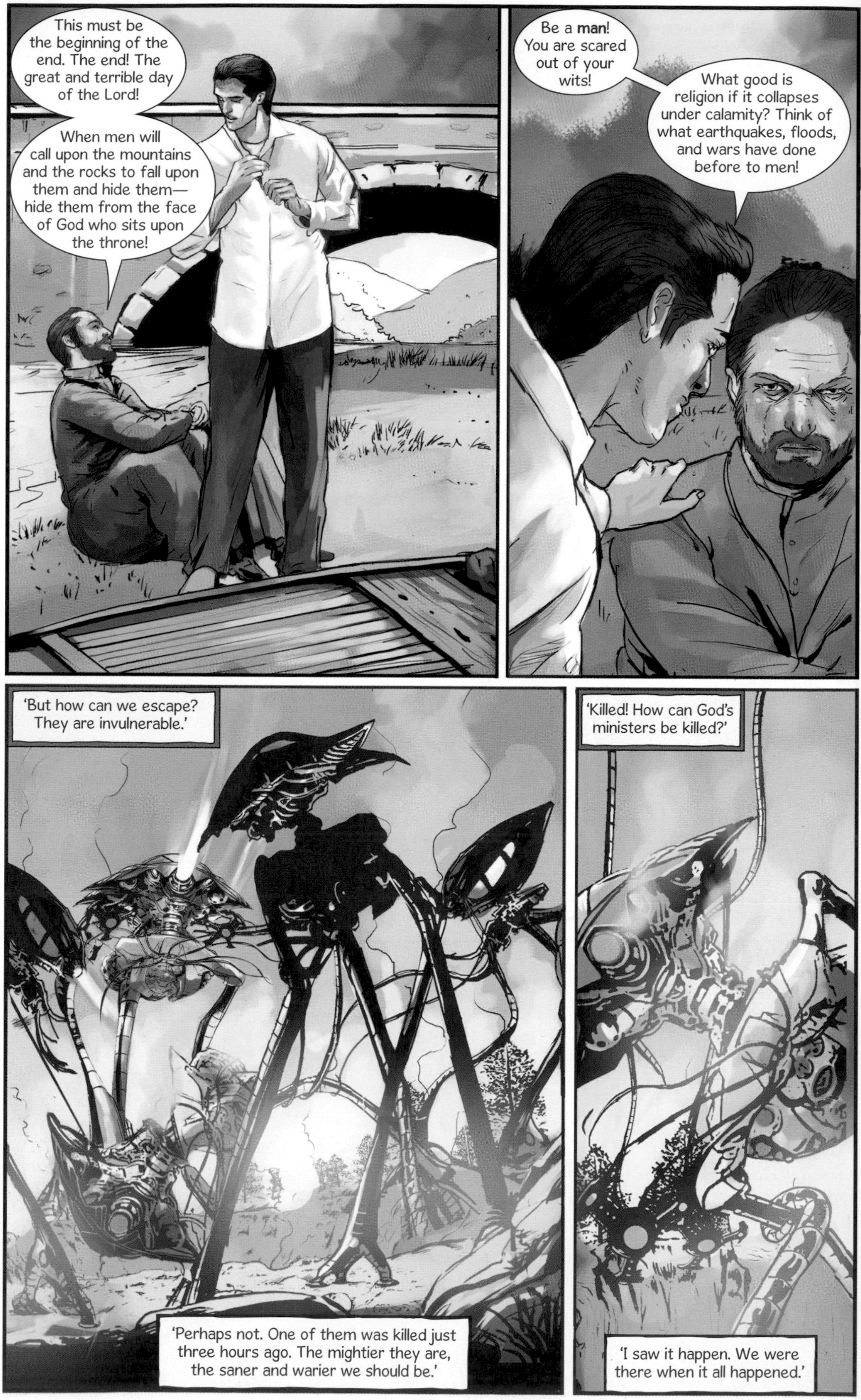

This must be the beginning of the end. The end! The great and terrible day of the Lord!
When men will call upon the mountains and the rocks to fall upon them and hide them—hide them from the face of God who sits upon the throne!
Be a **man**! You are scared out of your wits!
What good is religion if it collapses under calamity? Think of what earthquakes, floods, and wars have done before to men!
'But how can we escape? They are invulnerable.'
'Perhaps not. One of them was killed just three hours ago. The mightier they are, the saner and warier we should be.'
'Killed! How can God's ministers be killed?'
'I saw it happen. We were there when it all happened.'

Meanwhile, the Martians remained busy with preparations in the Horsell pit that day.

The Martians are over there. Their advance has only been temporarily halted.

AAAAIIIEE

BLAAM

Even as I spoke, from beyond the low hills across the water came the dull resonance of distant guns and weird crying.

We had better follow this path northward.

The Ripley gunners fired one wild, premature, ineffectual volley, and bolted on horse and foot through the deserted village.

A Martian walked serenely over to its guns, stepped gingerly among them, and came upon the guns at Painshill Park, which it destroyed.

The Martians were moving, as it seemed, upon a cloud, for a milky mist covered the fields and rose to the sky.

We then hurried wearily and painfully along the road.

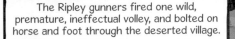

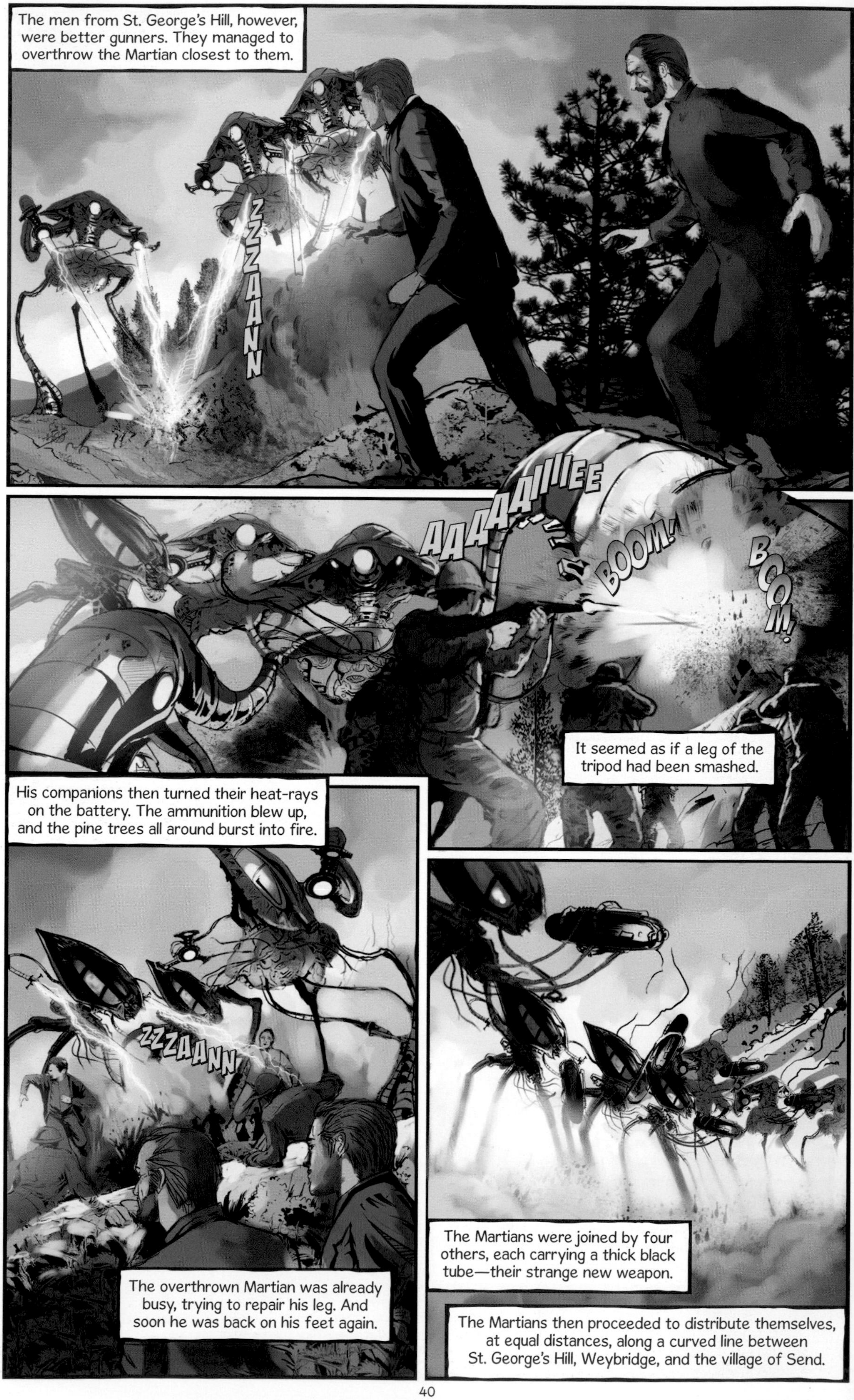
The men from St. George's Hill, however, were better gunners. They managed to overthrow the Martian closest to them.
ZZZAANN
AAAAAIIIIEE
BOOM!
BOOM!
It seemed as if a leg of the tripod had been smashed.
His companions then turned their heat-rays on the battery. The ammunition blew up, and the pine trees all around burst into fire.
ZZZAANN
The overthrown Martian was already busy, trying to repair his leg. And soon he was back on his feet again.
The Martians were joined by four others, each carrying a thick black tube—their strange new weapon.
The Martians then proceeded to distribute themselves, at equal distances, along a curved line between St. George's Hill, Weybridge, and the village of Send.

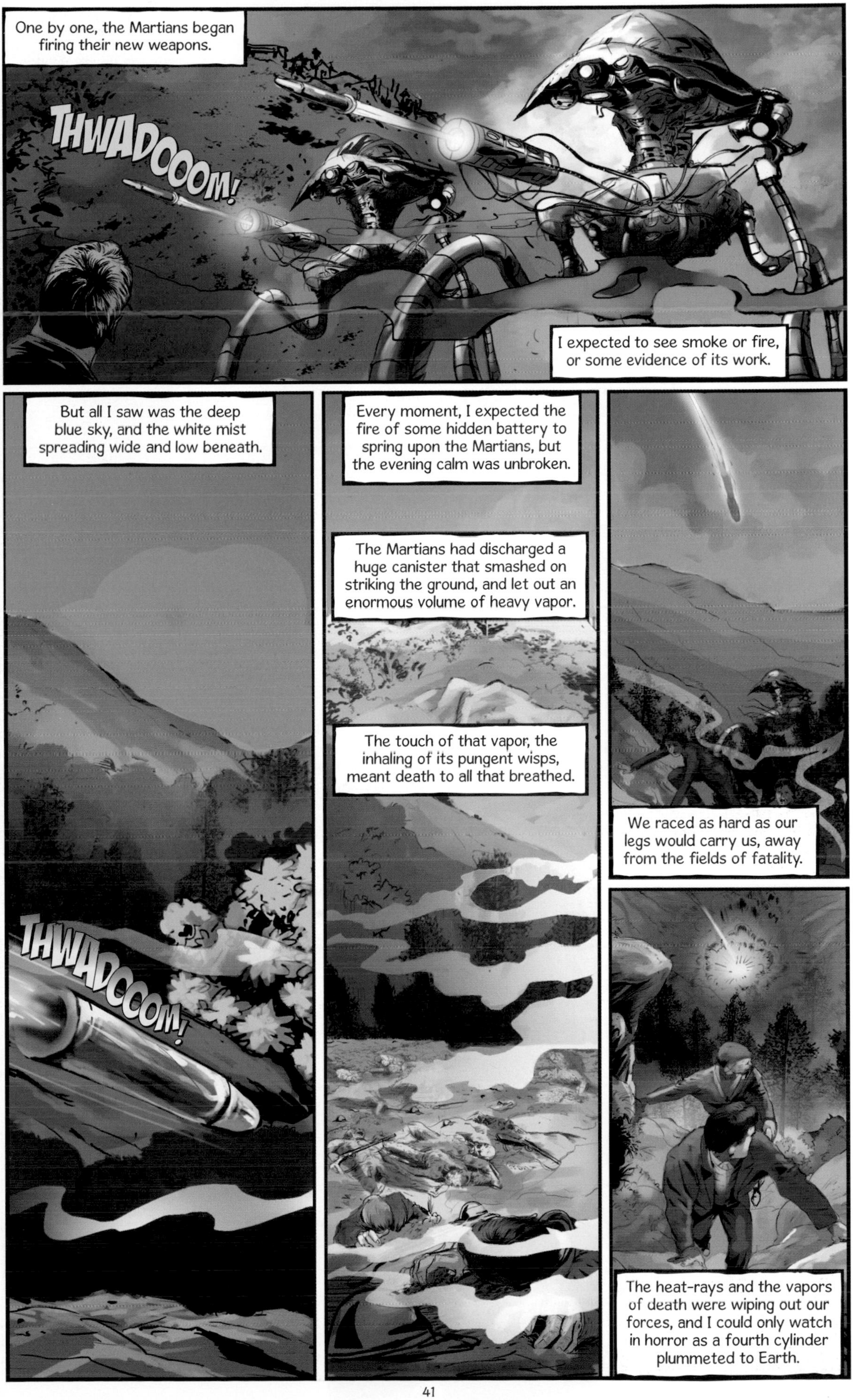

One by one, the Martians began firing their new weapons.
THWADOOOM!
I expected to see smoke or fire, or some evidence of its work.
But all I saw was the deep blue sky, and the white mist spreading wide and low beneath.
THWADOOOM!
Every moment, I expected the fire of some hidden battery to spring upon the Martians, but the evening calm was unbroken.
The Martians had discharged a huge canister that smashed on striking the ground, and let out an enormous volume of heavy vapor.
The touch of that vapor, the inhaling of its pungent wisps, meant death to all that breathed.
We raced as hard as our legs would carry us, away from the fields of fatality.
The heat-rays and the vapors of death were wiping out our forces, and I could only watch in horror as a fourth cylinder plummeted to Earth.

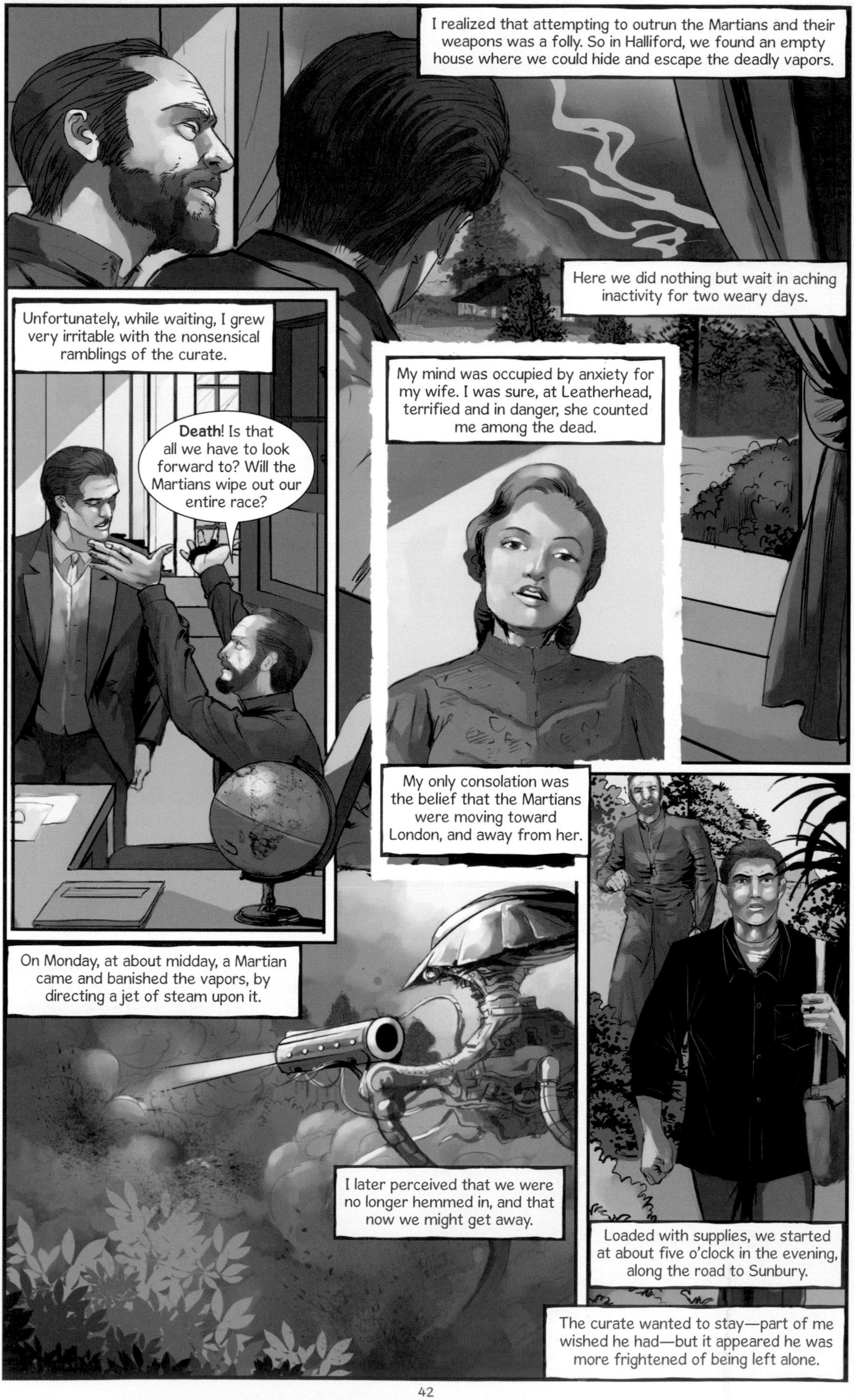
I realized that attempting to outrun the Martians and their weapons was a folly. So in Halliford, we found an empty house where we could hide and escape the deadly vapors.
Here we did nothing but wait in aching inactivity for two weary days.
Unfortunately, while waiting, I grew very irritable with the nonsensical ramblings of the curate.
Death! Is that all we have to look forward to? Will the Martians wipe out our entire race?
My mind was occupied by anxiety for my wife. I was sure, at Leatherhead, terrified and in danger, she counted me among the dead.
My only consolation was the belief that the Martians were moving toward London, and away from her.
On Monday, at about midday, a Martian came and banished the vapors, by directing a jet of steam upon it.
I later perceived that we were no longer hemmed in, and that now we might get away.
Loaded with supplies, we started at about five o'clock in the evening, along the road to Sunbury.
The curate wanted to stay—part of me wished he had—but it appeared he was more frightened of being left alone.

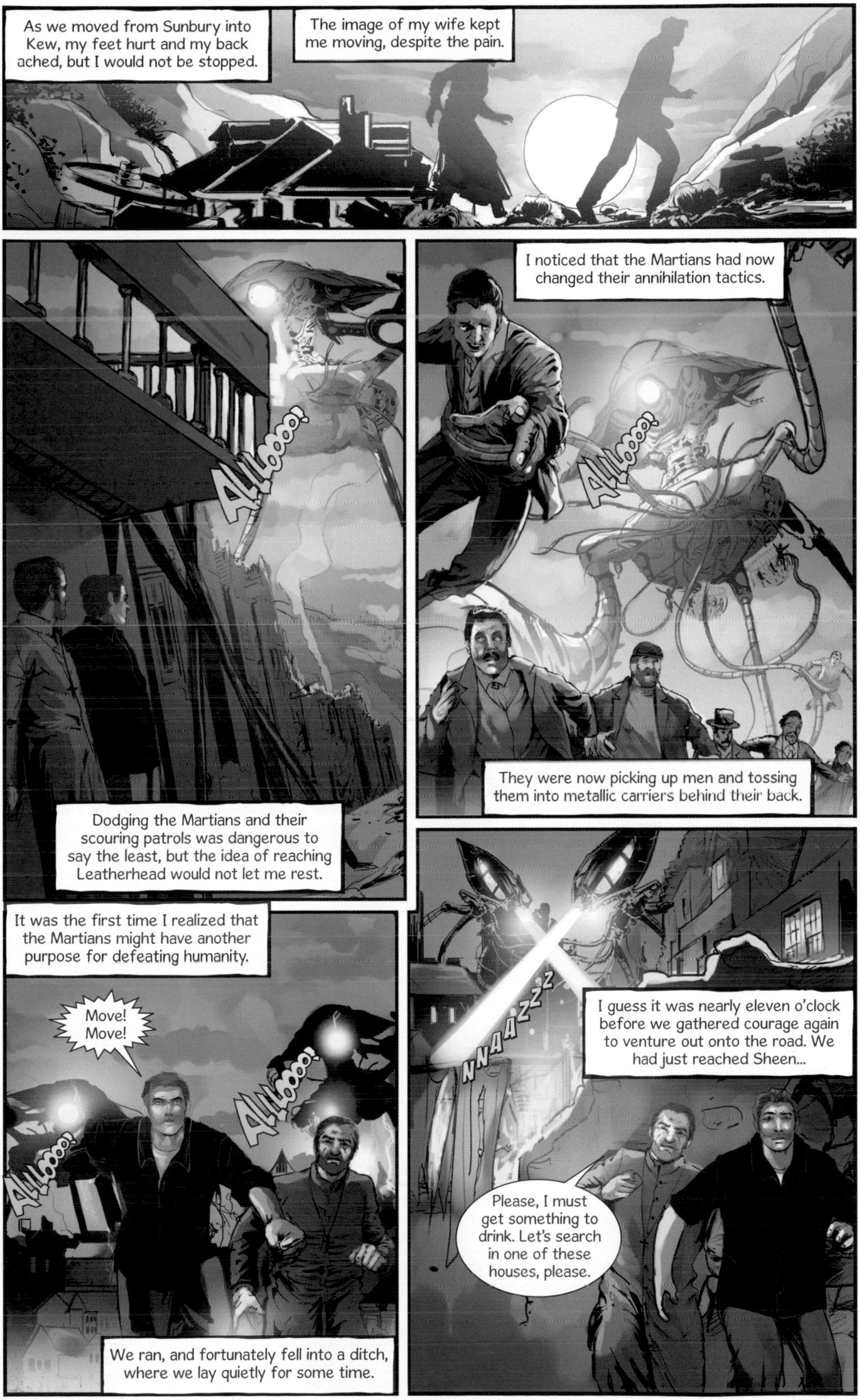
As we moved from Sunbury into Kew, my feet hurt and my back ached, but I would not be stopped.
The image of my wife kept me moving, despite the pain.
ALLOOOO!
Dodging the Martians and their scouring patrols was dangerous to say the least, but the idea of reaching Leatherhead would not let me rest.
I noticed that the Martians had now changed their annihilation tactics.
ALLOOOO!
They were now picking up men and tossing them into metallic carriers behind their back.
It was the first time I realized that the Martians might have another purpose for defeating humanity.
Move! Move!
ALLOOOO!
ALLOOOO!
We ran, and fortunately fell into a ditch, where we lay quietly for some time.
NNAAAZZZ
I guess it was nearly eleven o'clock before we gathered courage again to venture out onto the road. We had just reached Sheen...
Please, I must get something to drink. Let's search in one of these houses, please.

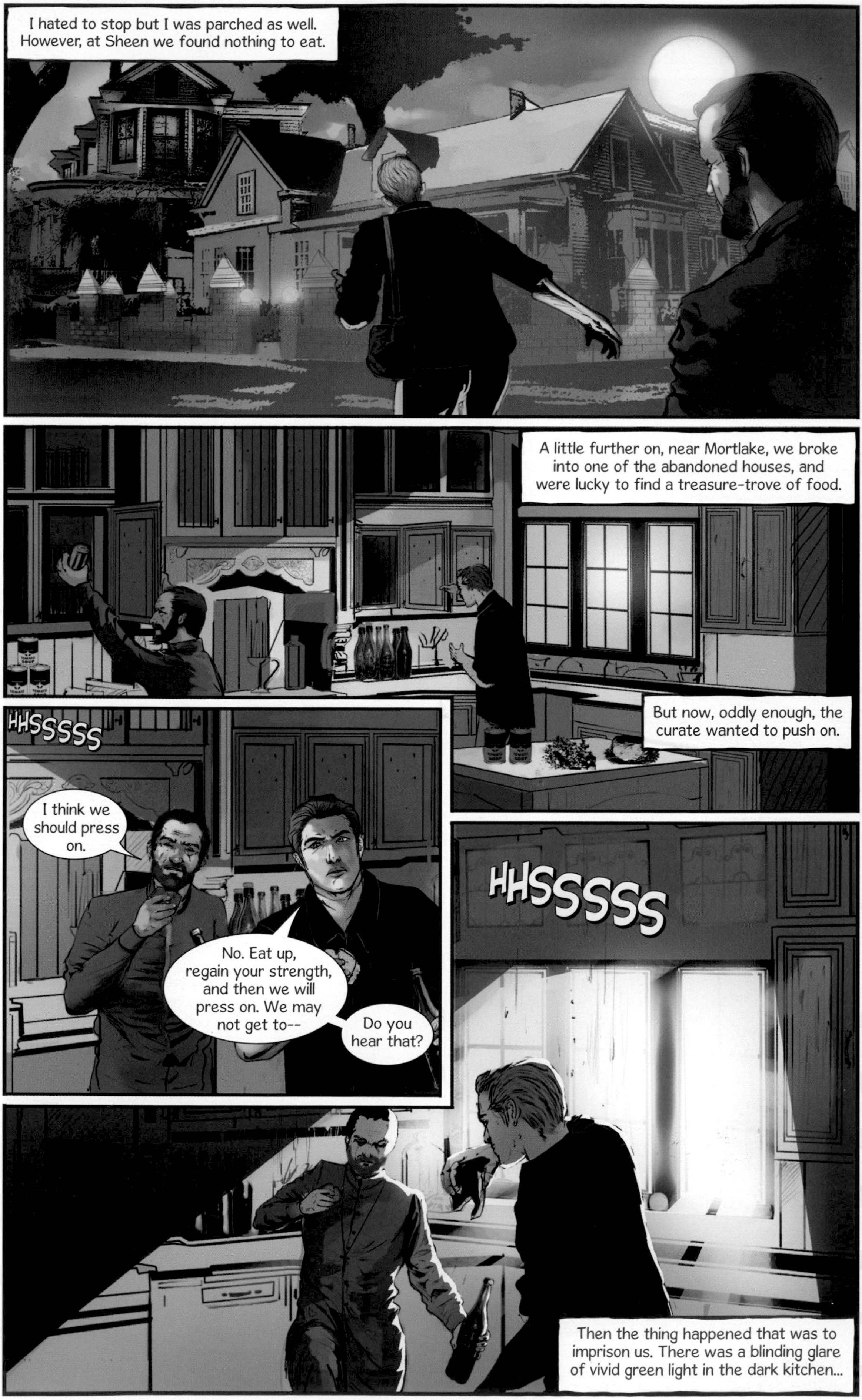
I hated to stop but I was parched as well. However, at Sheen we found nothing to eat.
A little further on, near Mortlake, we broke into one of the abandoned houses, and were lucky to find a treasure-trove of food.
But now, oddly enough, the curate wanted to push on.
HHSSSSS
I think we should press on.
No. Eat up, regain your strength, and then we will press on. We may not get to--
Do you hear that?
HHSSSSS
Then the thing happened that was to imprison us. There was a blinding glare of vivid green light in the dark kitchen...

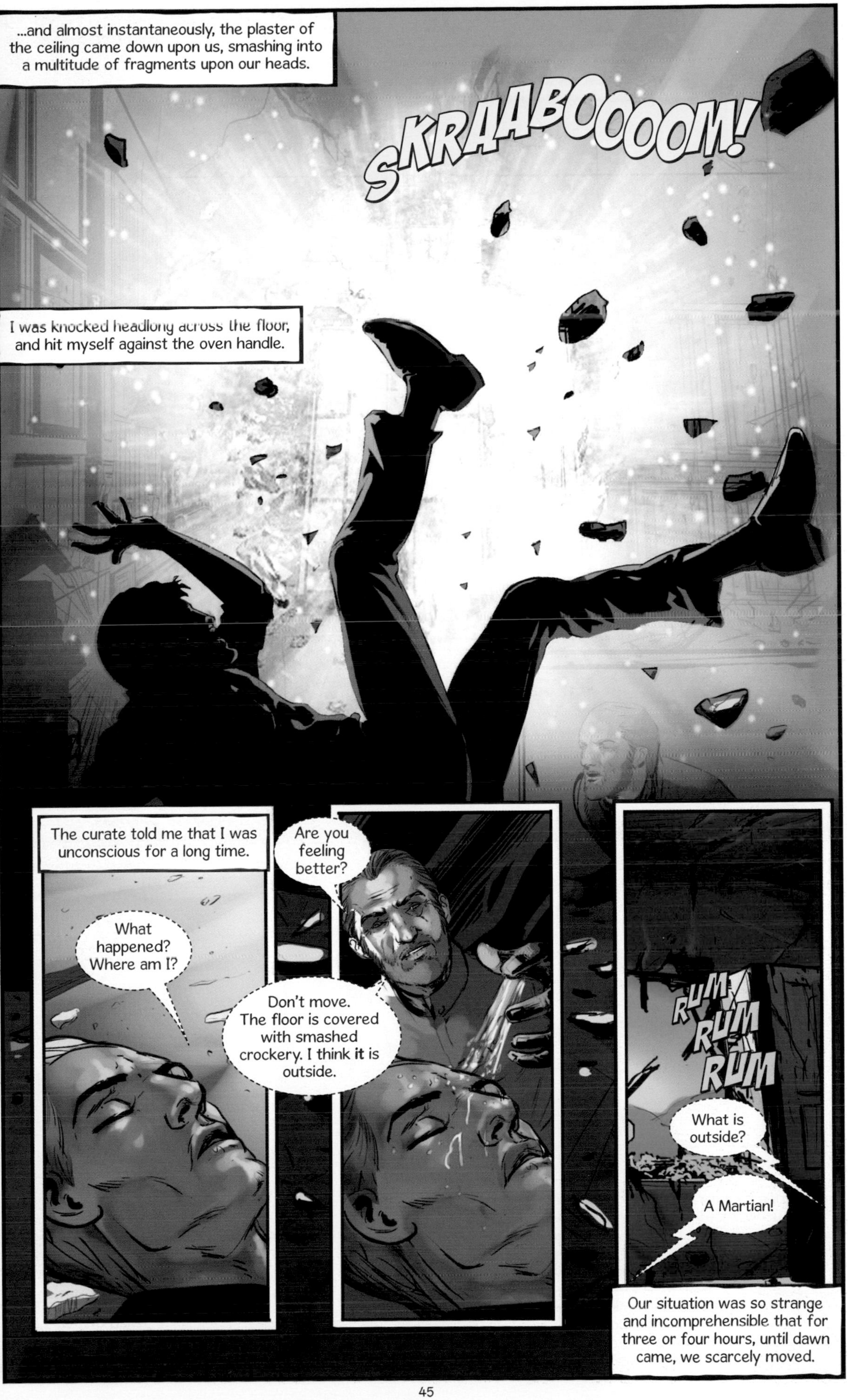

...and almost instantaneously, the plaster of the ceiling came down upon us, smashing into a multitude of fragments upon our heads.
SKRAABOOOOOM!
I was knocked headlong across the floor, and hit myself against the oven handle.
The curate told me that I was unconscious for a long time.
What happened? Where am I?
Are you feeling better?
Don't move. The floor is covered with smashed crockery. I think **it** is outside.
RUM RUM RUM
What is outside?
A Martian!
Our situation was so strange and incomprehensible that for three or four hours, until dawn came, we scarcely moved.

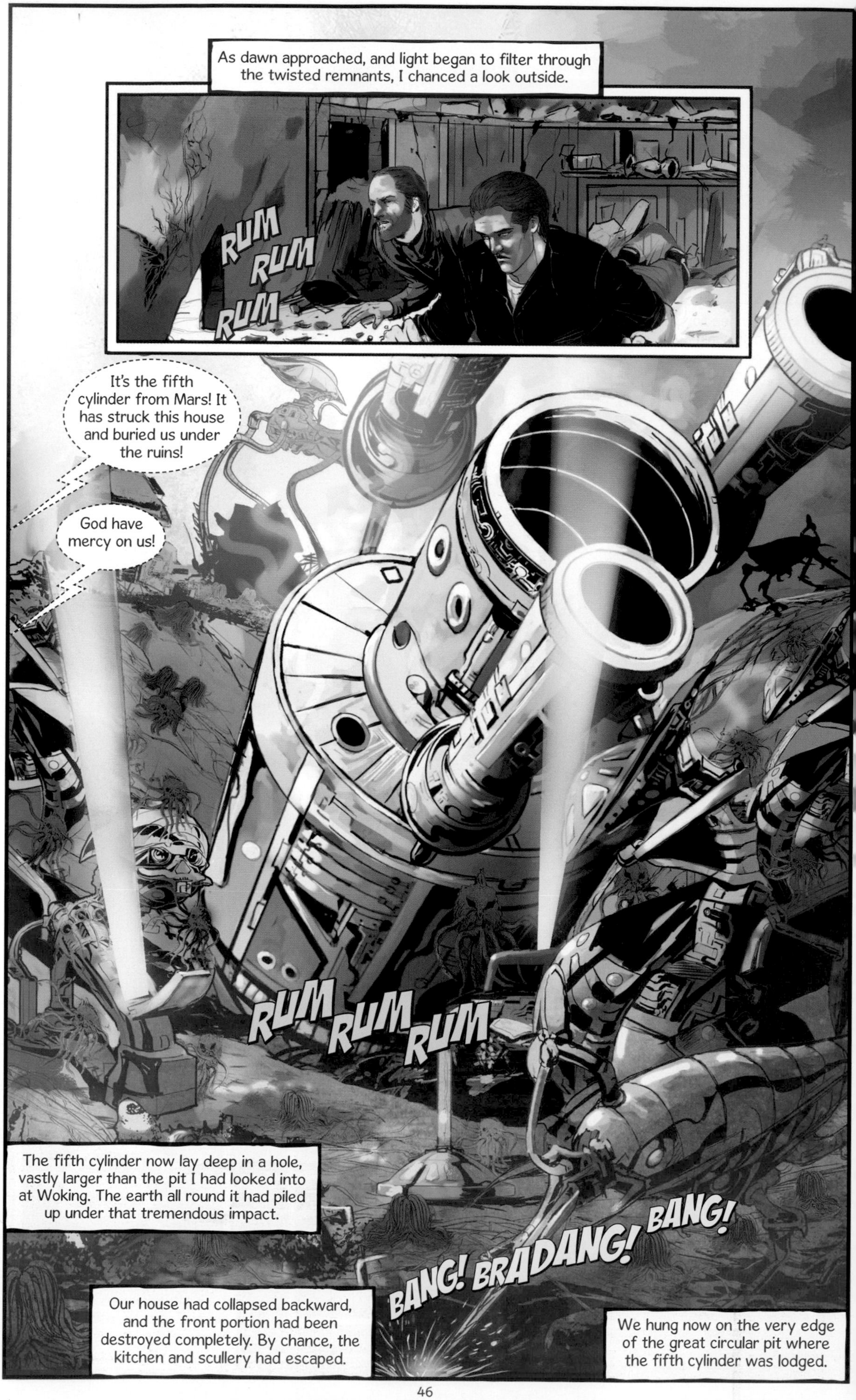
As dawn approached, and light began to filter through the twisted remnants, I chanced a look outside.
RUM RUM RUM
It's the fifth cylinder from Mars! It has struck this house and buried us under the ruins!
God have mercy on us!
RUM RUM RUM
The fifth cylinder now lay deep in a hole, vastly larger than the pit I had looked into at Woking. The earth all round it had piled up under that tremendous impact.
Our house had collapsed backward, and the front portion had been destroyed completely. By chance, the kitchen and scullery had escaped.
BANG! BRADANG! BANG!
We hung now on the very edge of the great circular pit where the fifth cylinder was lodged.

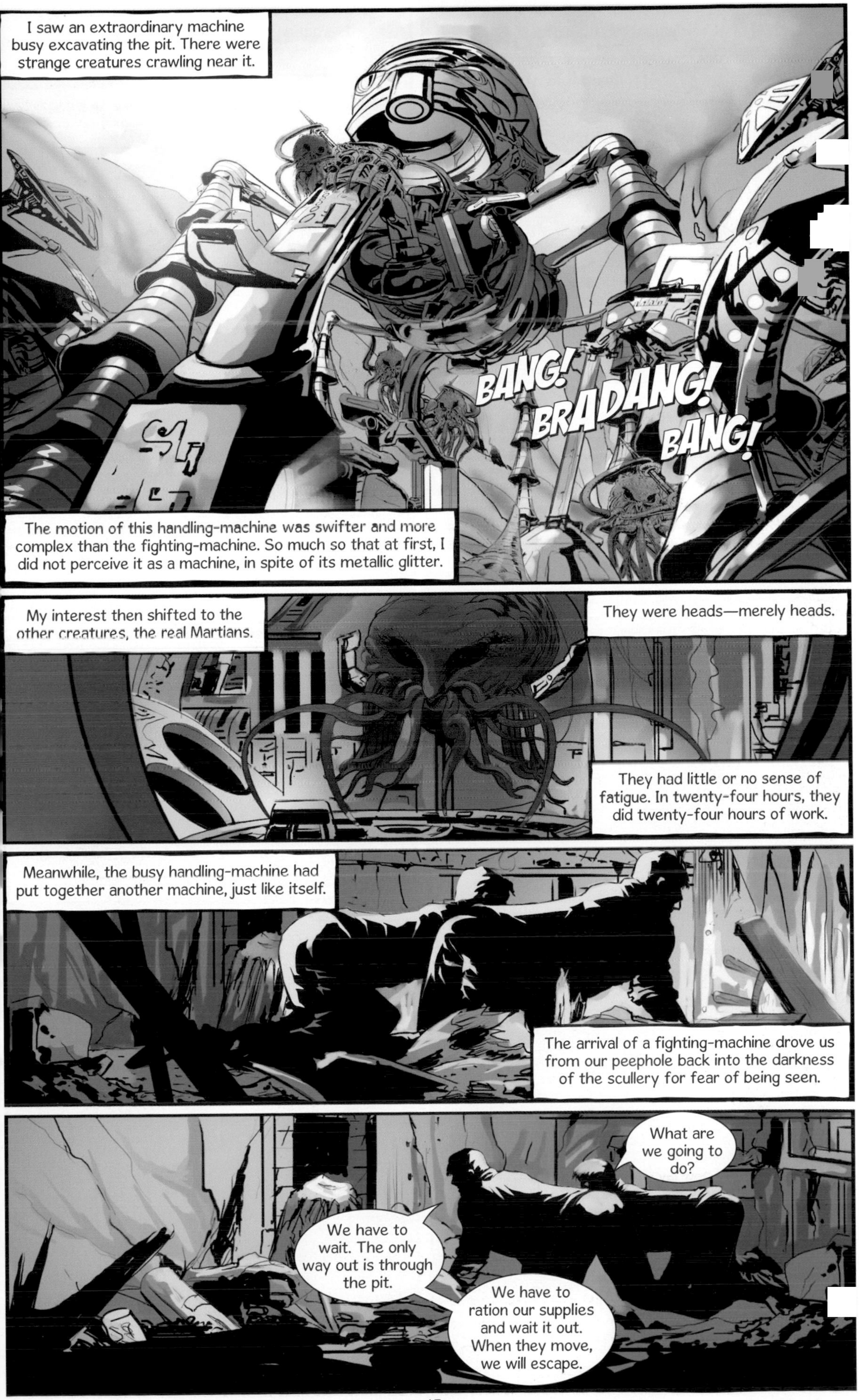
I saw an extraordinary machine busy excavating the pit. There were strange creatures crawling near it.
BANG!
BRADANG!
BANG!
The motion of this handling-machine was swifter and more complex than the fighting-machine. So much so that at first, I did not perceive it as a machine, in spite of its metallic glitter.
My interest then shifted to the other creatures, the real Martians.
They were heads—merely heads.
They had little or no sense of fatigue. In twenty-four hours, they did twenty-four hours of work.
Meanwhile, the busy handling-machine had put together another machine, just like itself.
The arrival of a fighting-machine drove us from our peephole back into the darkness of the scullery for fear of being seen.
What are we going to do?
We have to wait. The only way out is through the pit.
We have to ration our supplies and wait it out. When they move, we will escape.

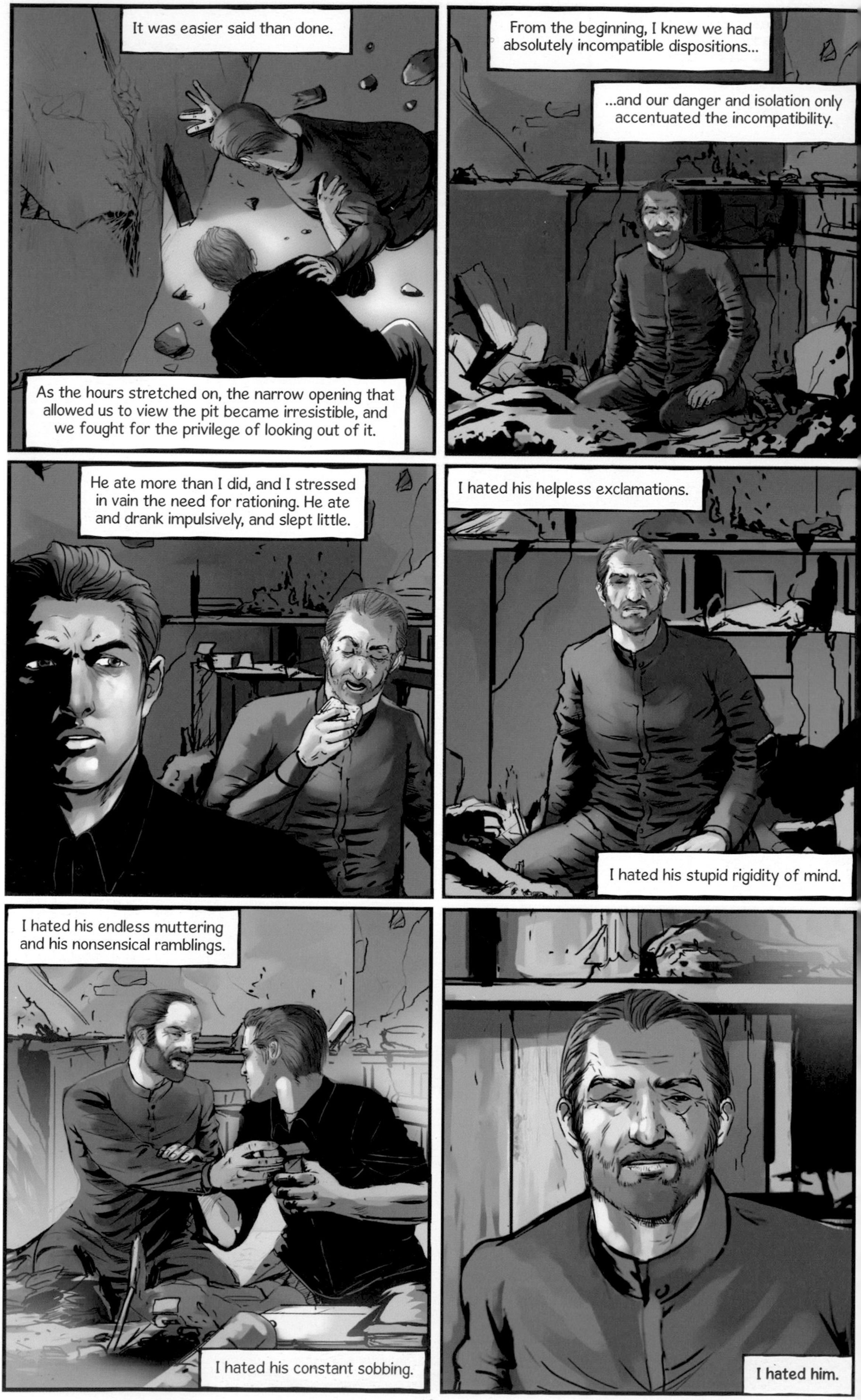

It was easier said than done.
As the hours stretched on, the narrow opening that allowed us to view the pit became irresistible, and we fought for the privilege of looking out of it.
From the beginning, I knew we had absolutely incompatible dispositions...
...and our danger and isolation only accentuated the incompatibility.
He ate more than I did, and I stressed in vain the need for rationing. He ate and drank impulsively, and slept little.
I hated his helpless exclamations.
I hated his stupid rigidity of mind.
I hated his endless muttering and his nonsensical ramblings.
I hated his constant sobbing.
I hated him.

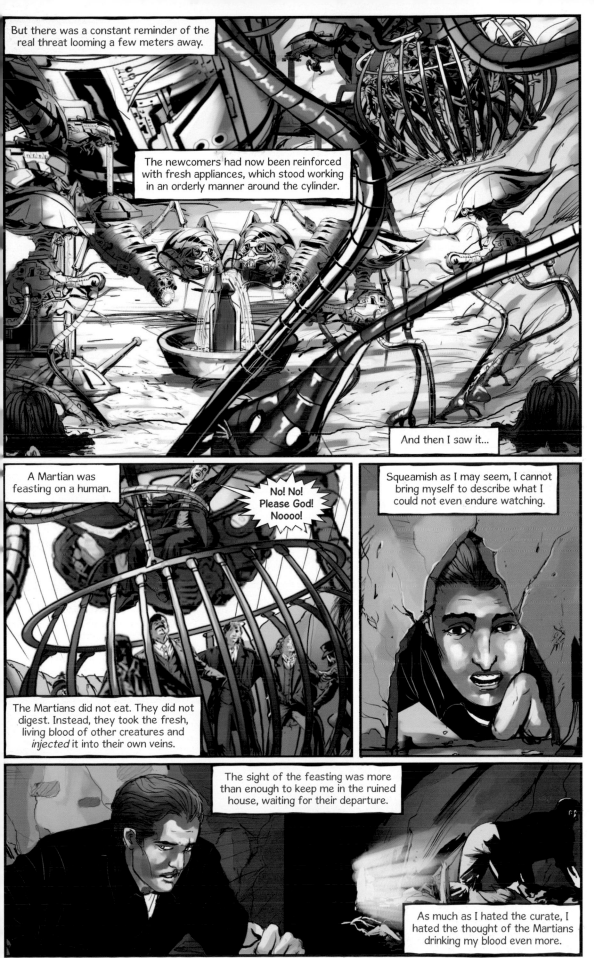

But there was a constant reminder of the real threat looming a few meters away.

The newcomers had now been reinforced with fresh appliances, which stood working in an orderly manner around the cylinder.

And then I saw it...

A Martian was feasting on a human.

No! No! Please God! Noooo!

The Martians did not eat. They did not digest. Instead, they took the fresh, living blood of other creatures and *injected* it into their own veins.

Squeamish as I may seem, I cannot bring myself to describe what I could not even endure watching.

The sight of the feasting was more than enough to keep me in the ruined house, waiting for their departure.

As much as I hated the curate, I hated the thought of the Martians drinking my blood even more.

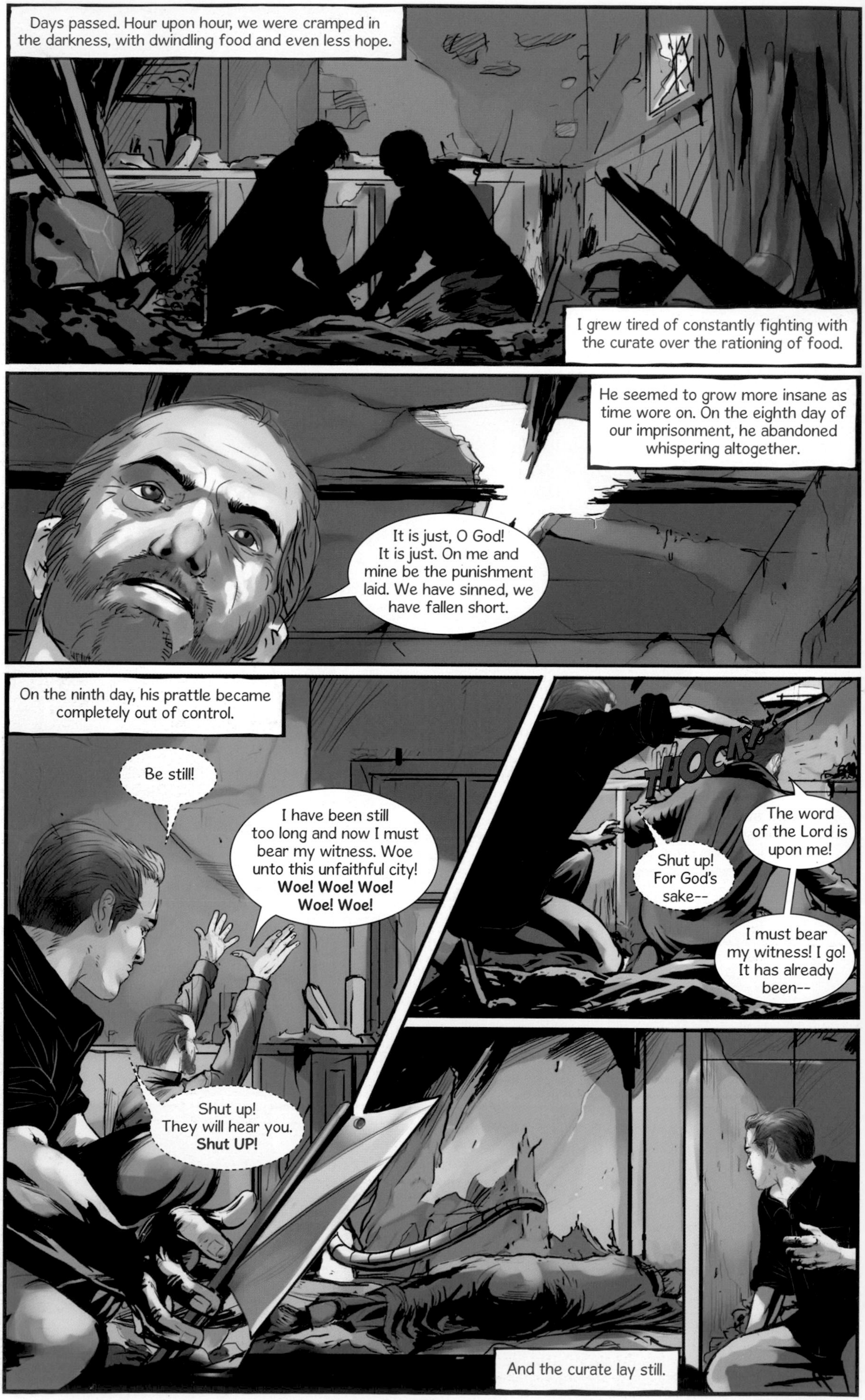
Days passed. Hour upon hour, we were cramped in the darkness, with dwindling food and even less hope.
I grew tired of constantly fighting with the curate over the rationing of food.
He seemed to grow more insane as time wore on. On the eighth day of our imprisonment, he abandoned whispering altogether.
It is just, O God! It is just. On me and mine be the punishment laid. We have sinned, we have fallen short.
On the ninth day, his prattle became completely out of control.
Be still!
I have been still too long and now I must bear my witness. Woe unto this unfaithful city! Woe! Woe! Woe! Woe! Woe!
Shut up! They will hear you. Shut UP!
THOCK!
The word of the Lord is upon me!
Shut up! For God's sake--
I must bear my witness! I go! It has already been--
And the curate lay still.

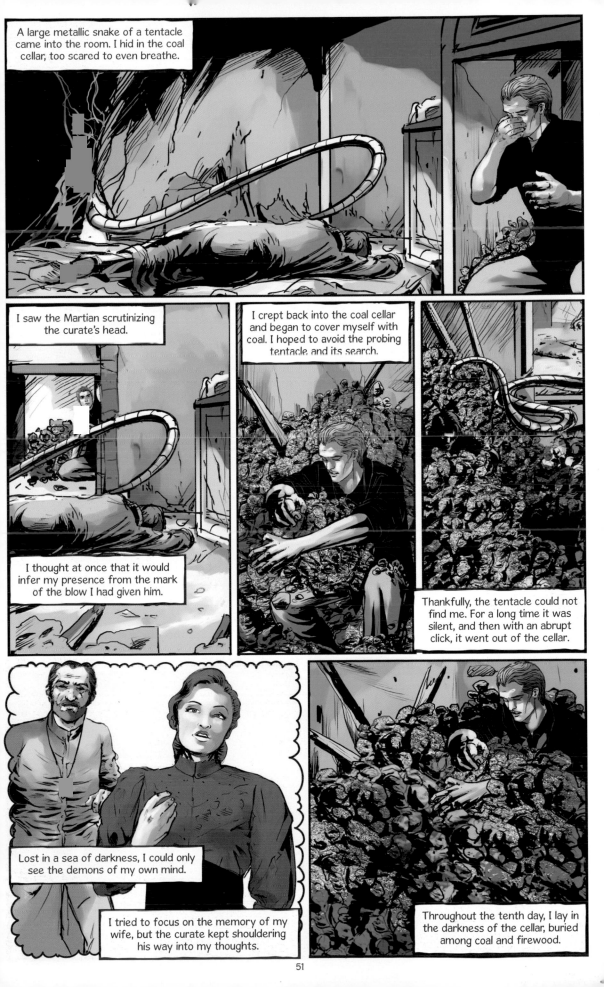

A large metallic snake of a tentacle came into the room. I hid in the coal cellar, too scared to even breathe.

I saw the Martian scrutinizing the curate's head.

I thought at once that it would infer my presence from the mark of the blow I had given him.

I crept back into the coal cellar and began to cover myself with coal. I hoped to avoid the probing tentacle and its search.

Thankfully, the tentacle could not find me. For a long time it was silent, and then with an abrupt click, it went out of the cellar.

Lost in a sea of darkness, I could only see the demons of my own mind.

I tried to focus on the memory of my wife, but the curate kept shouldering his way into my thoughts.

Throughout the tenth day, I lay in the darkness of the cellar, buried among coal and firewood.

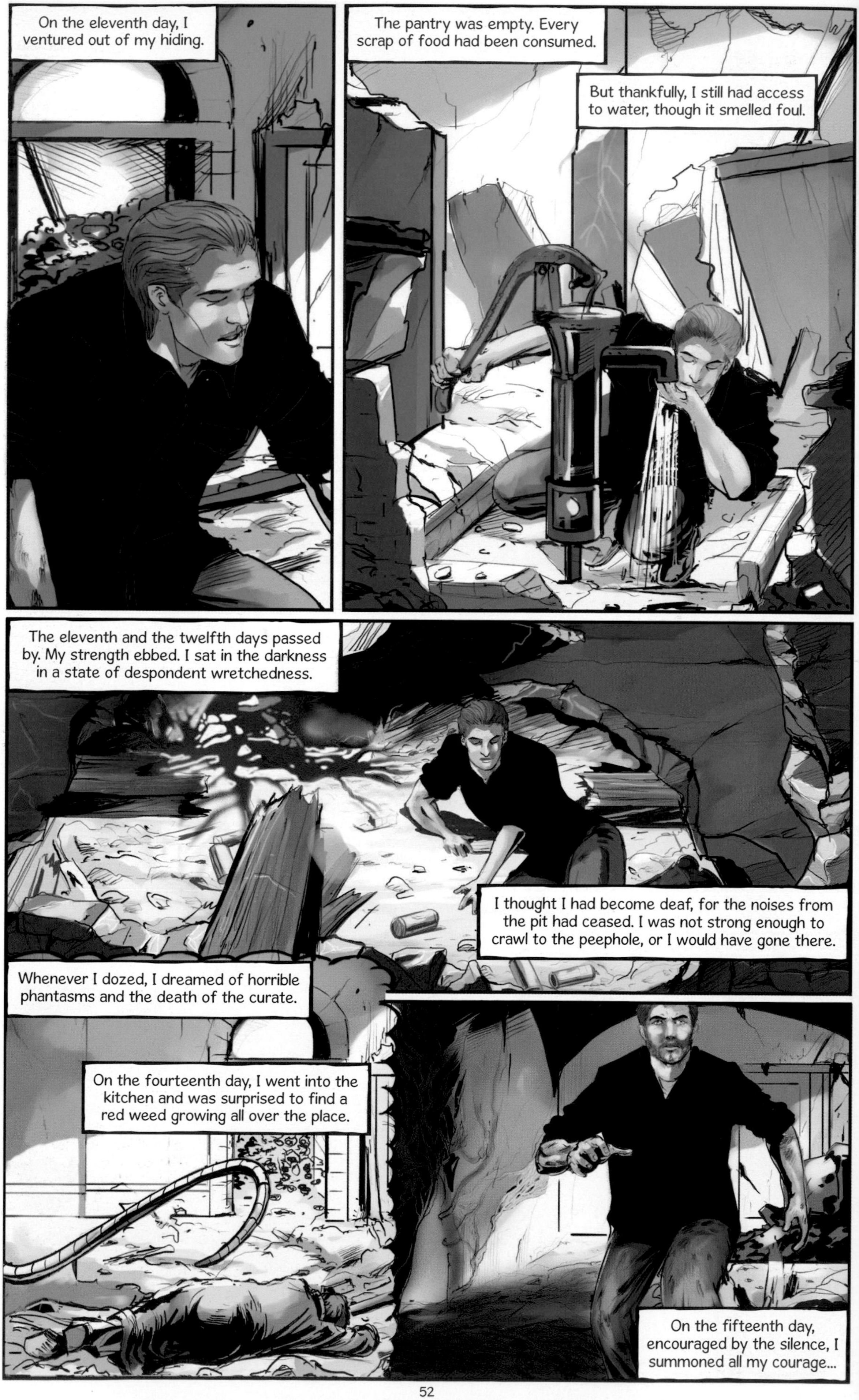
On the eleventh day, I ventured out of my hiding.
The pantry was empty. Every scrap of food had been consumed.
But thankfully, I still had access to water, though it smelled foul.
The eleventh and the twelfth days passed by. My strength ebbed. I sat in the darkness in a state of despondent wretchedness.
I thought I had become deaf, for the noises from the pit had ceased. I was not strong enough to crawl to the peephole, or I would have gone there.
Whenever I dozed, I dreamed of horrible phantasms and the death of the curate.
On the fourteenth day, I went into the kitchen and was surprised to find a red weed growing all over the place.
On the fifteenth day, encouraged by the silence, I summoned all my courage...

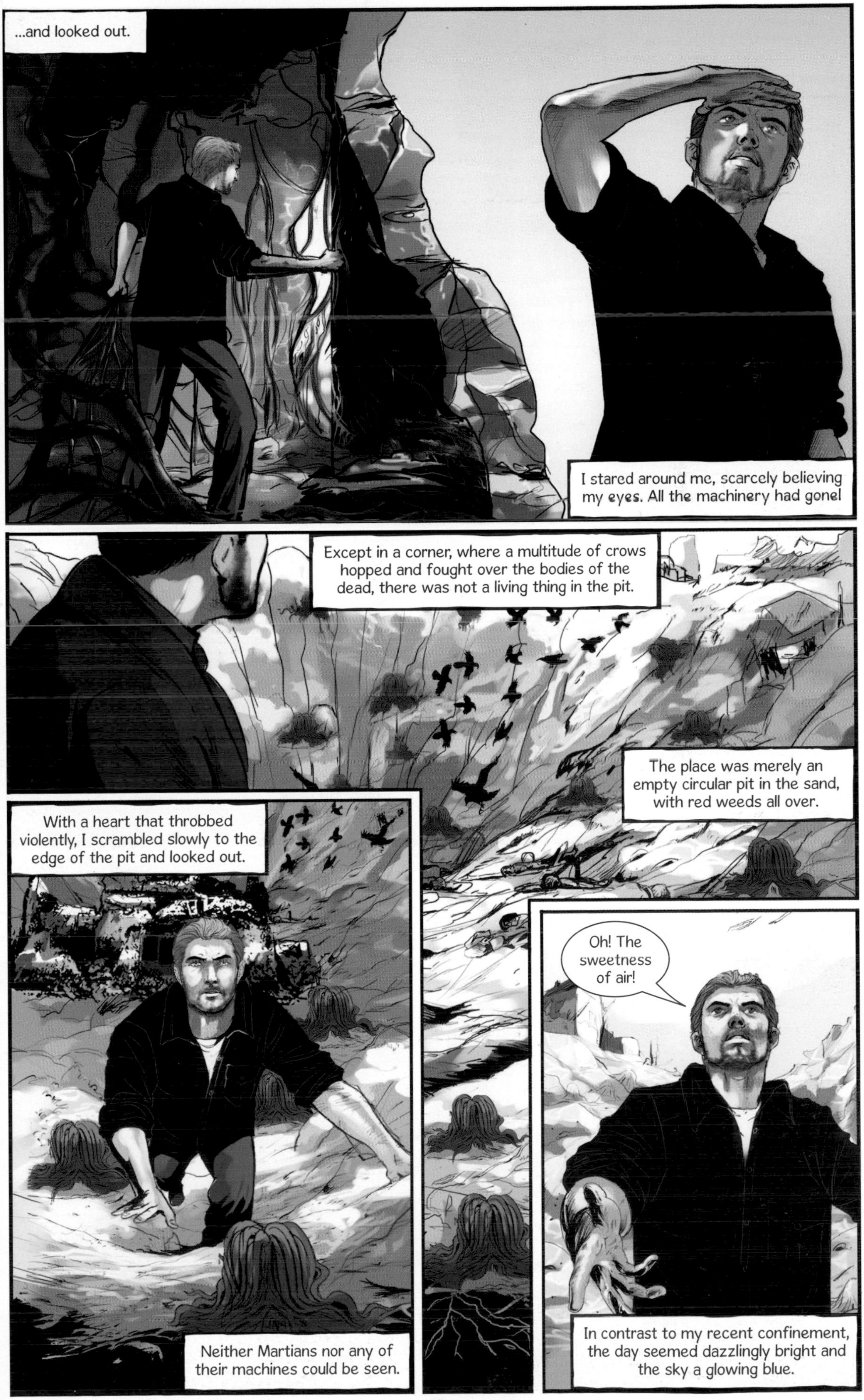

...and looked out.
I stared around me, scarcely believing my eyes. All the machinery had gone!
Except in a corner, where a multitude of crows hopped and fought over the bodies of the dead, there was not a living thing in the pit.
The place was merely an empty circular pit in the sand, with red weeds all over.
With a heart that throbbed violently, I scrambled slowly to the edge of the pit and looked out.
Neither Martians nor any of their machines could be seen.
Oh! The sweetness of air!
In contrast to my recent confinement, the day seemed dazzlingly bright and the sky a glowing blue.

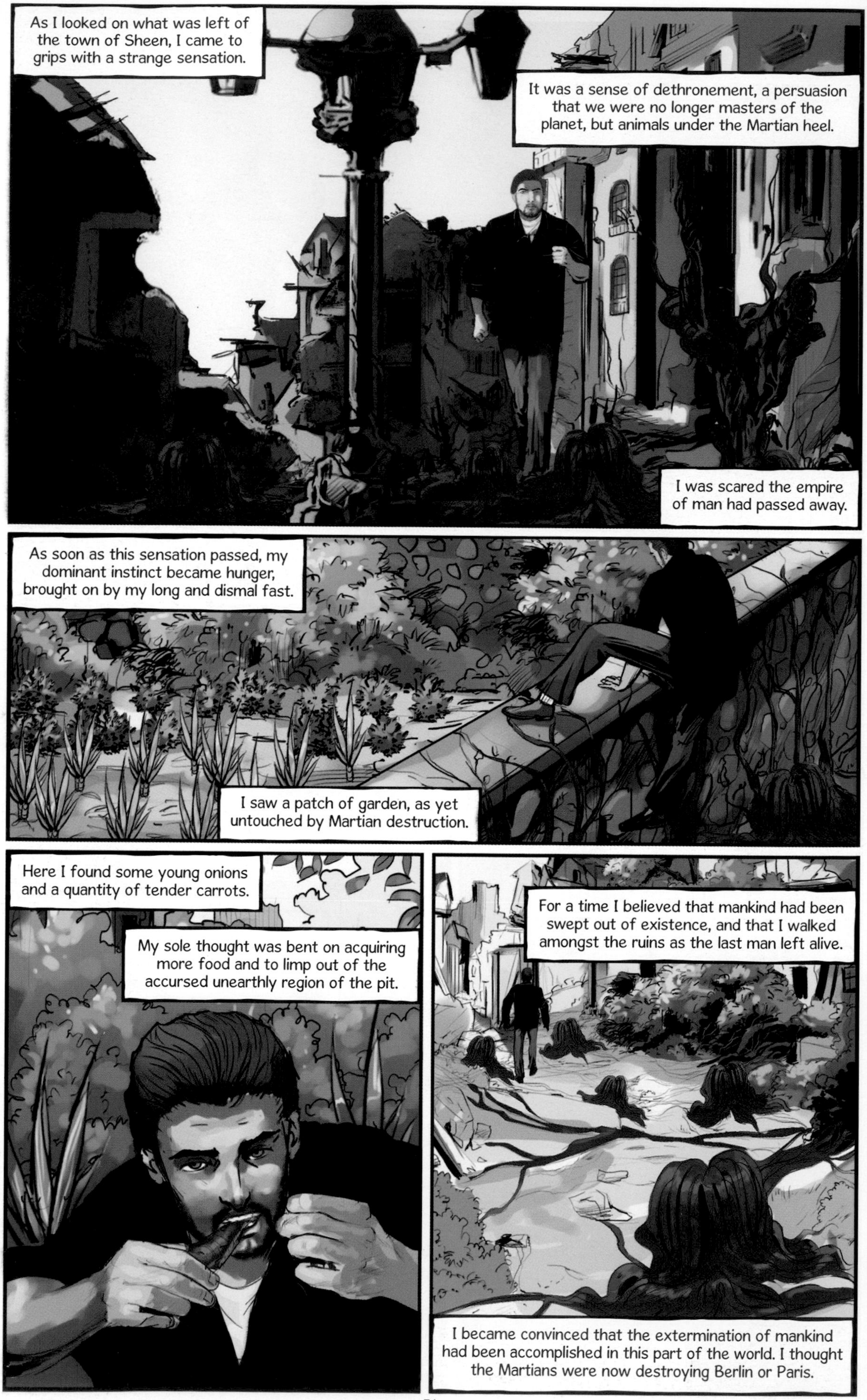
As I looked on what was left of the town of Sheen, I came to grips with a strange sensation.
It was a sense of dethronement, a persuasion that we were no longer masters of the planet, but animals under the Martian heel.
I was scared the empire of man had passed away.
As soon as this sensation passed, my dominant instinct became hunger, brought on by my long and dismal fast.
I saw a patch of garden, as yet untouched by Martian destruction.
Here I found some young onions and a quantity of tender carrots.
My sole thought was bent on acquiring more food and to limp out of the accursed unearthly region of the pit.
For a time I believed that mankind had been swept out of existence, and that I walked amongst the ruins as the last man left alive.
I became convinced that the extermination of mankind had been accomplished in this part of the world. I thought the Martians were now destroying Berlin or Paris.

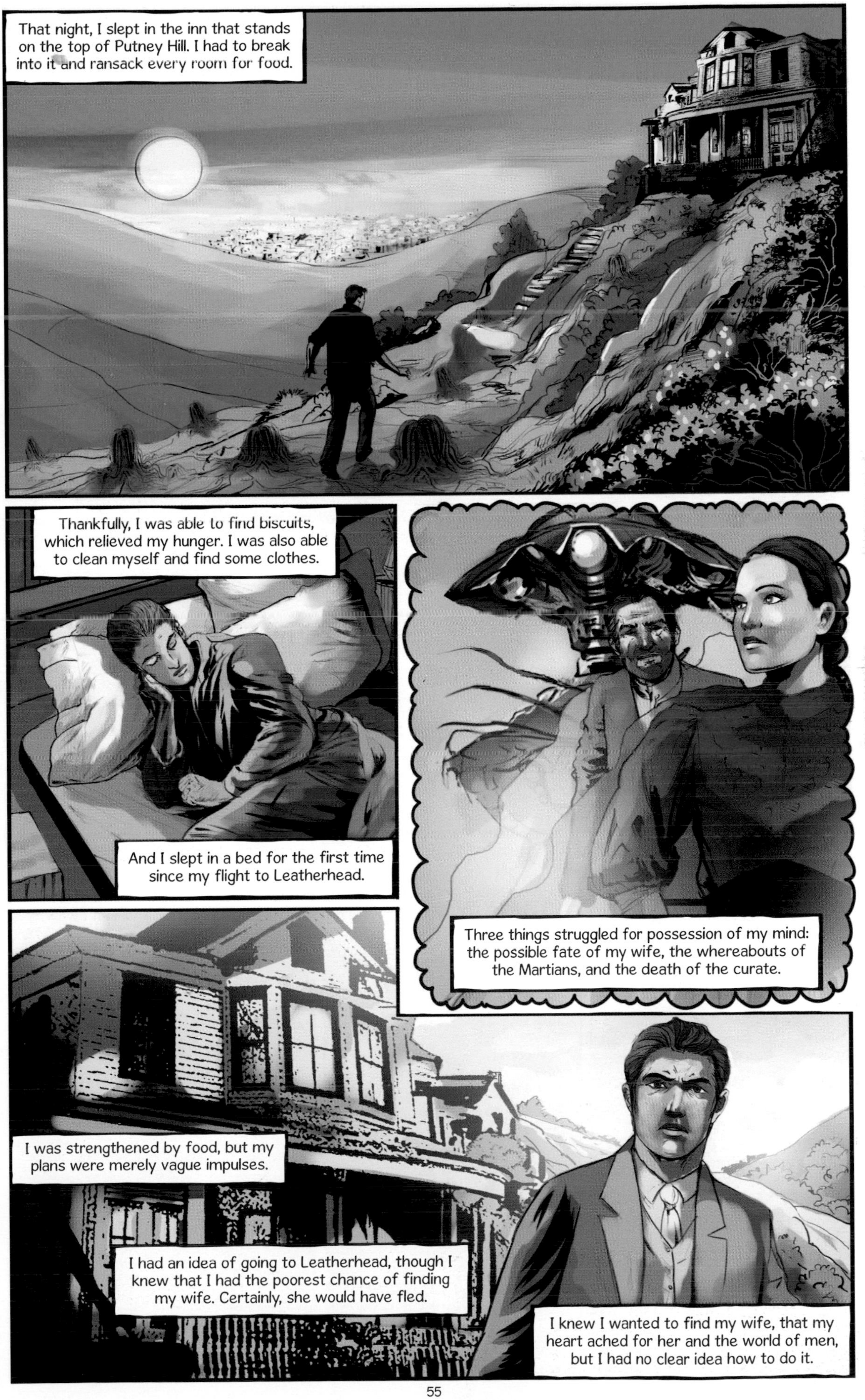
That night, I slept in the inn that stands on the top of Putney Hill. I had to break into it and ransack every room for food.
Thankfully, I was able to find biscuits, which relieved my hunger. I was also able to clean myself and find some clothes.
And I slept in a bed for the first time since my flight to Leatherhead.
Three things struggled for possession of my mind: the possible fate of my wife, the whereabouts of the Martians, and the death of the curate.
I was strengthened by food, but my plans were merely vague impulses.
I had an idea of going to Leatherhead, though I knew that I had the poorest chance of finding my wife. Certainly, she would have fled.
I knew I wanted to find my wife, that my heart ached for her and the world of men, but I had no clear idea how to do it.

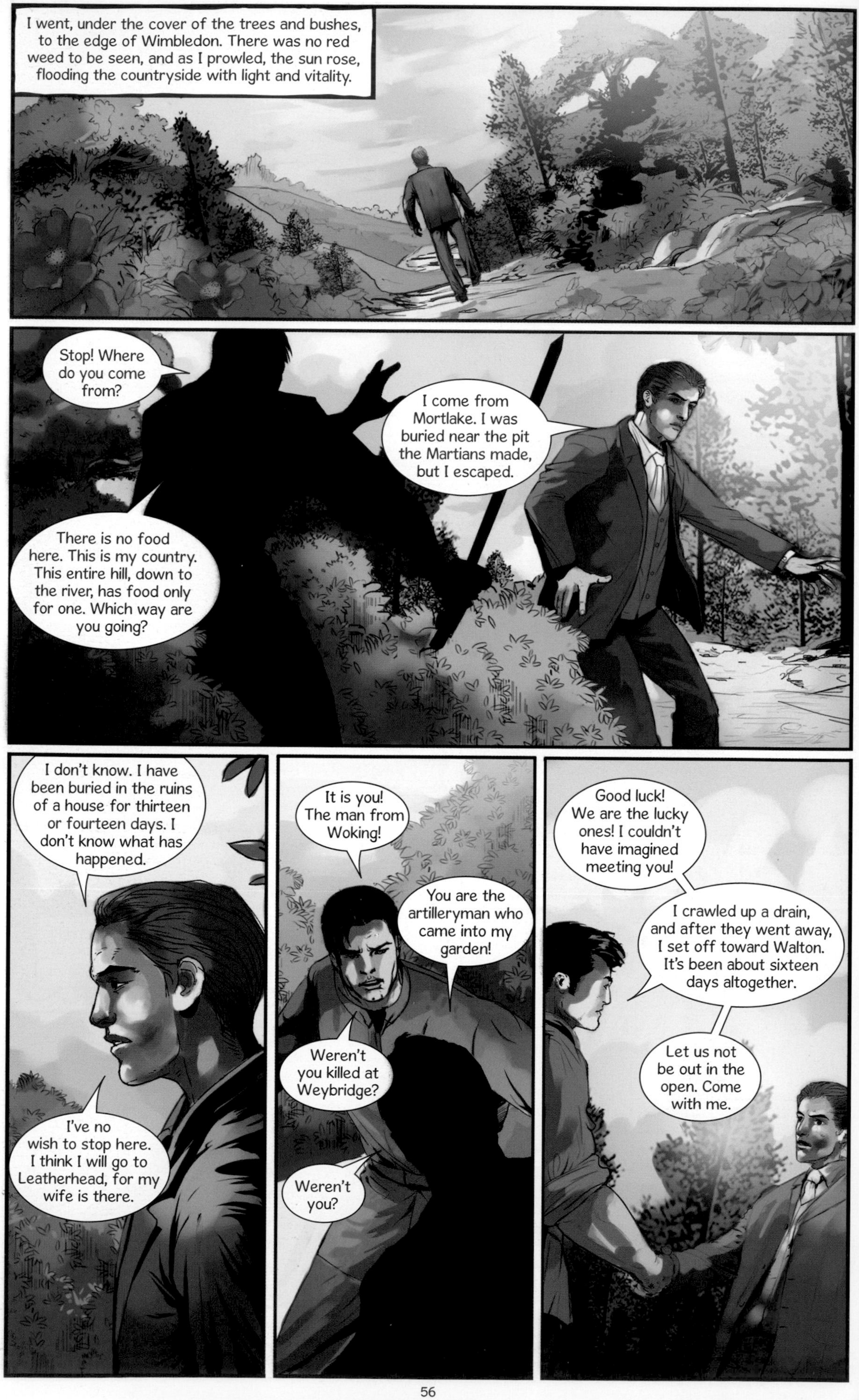

I went, under the cover of the trees and bushes, to the edge of Wimbledon. There was no red weed to be seen, and as I prowled, the sun rose, flooding the countryside with light and vitality.
Stop! Where do you come from?
I come from Mortlake. I was buried near the pit the Martians made, but I escaped.
There is no food here. This is my country. This entire hill, down to the river, has food only for one. Which way are you going?
I don't know. I have been buried in the ruins of a house for thirteen or fourteen days. I don't know what has happened.
I've no wish to stop here. I think I will go to Leatherhead, for my wife is there.
It is you! The man from Woking!
You are the artilleryman who came into my garden!
Weren't you killed at Weybridge?
Weren't you?
Good luck! We are the lucky ones! I couldn't have imagined meeting you!
I crawled up a drain, and after they went away, I set off toward Walton. It's been about sixteen days altogether.
Let us not be out in the open. Come with me.

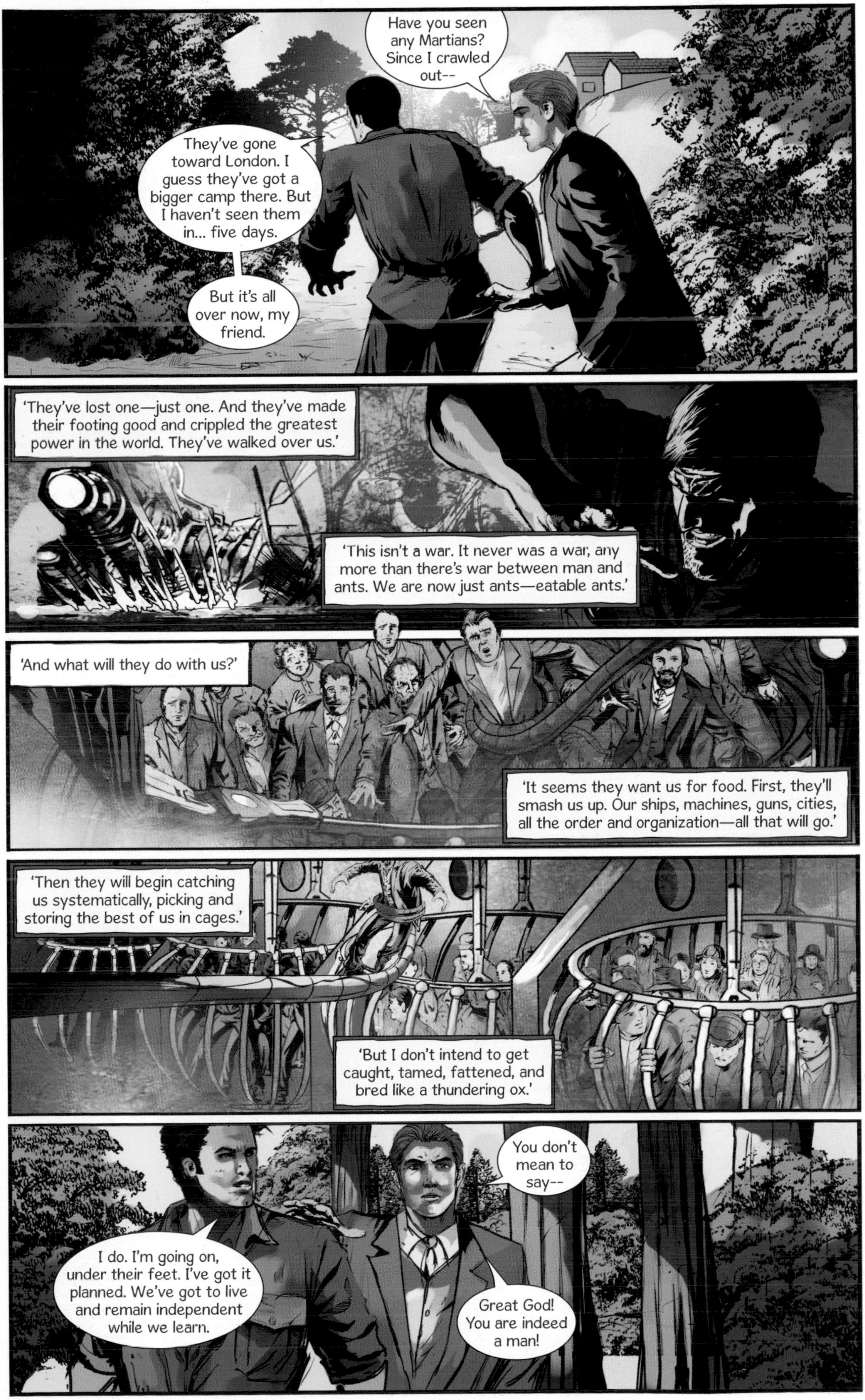
Have you seen any Martians? Since I crawled out--
They've gone toward London. I guess they've got a bigger camp there. But I haven't seen them in... five days.
But it's all over now, my friend.
'They've lost one—just one. And they've made their footing good and crippled the greatest power in the world. They've walked over us.'
'This isn't a war. It never was a war, any more than there's war between man and ants. We are now just ants—eatable ants.'
'And what will they do with us?'
'It seems they want us for food. First, they'll smash us up. Our ships, machines, guns, cities, all the order and organization—all that will go.'
'Then they will begin catching us systematically, picking and storing the best of us in cages.'
'But I don't intend to get caught, tamed, fattened, and bred like a thundering ox.'
You don't mean to say--
I do. I'm going on, under their feet. I've got it planned. We've got to live and remain independent while we learn.
Great God! You are indeed a man!

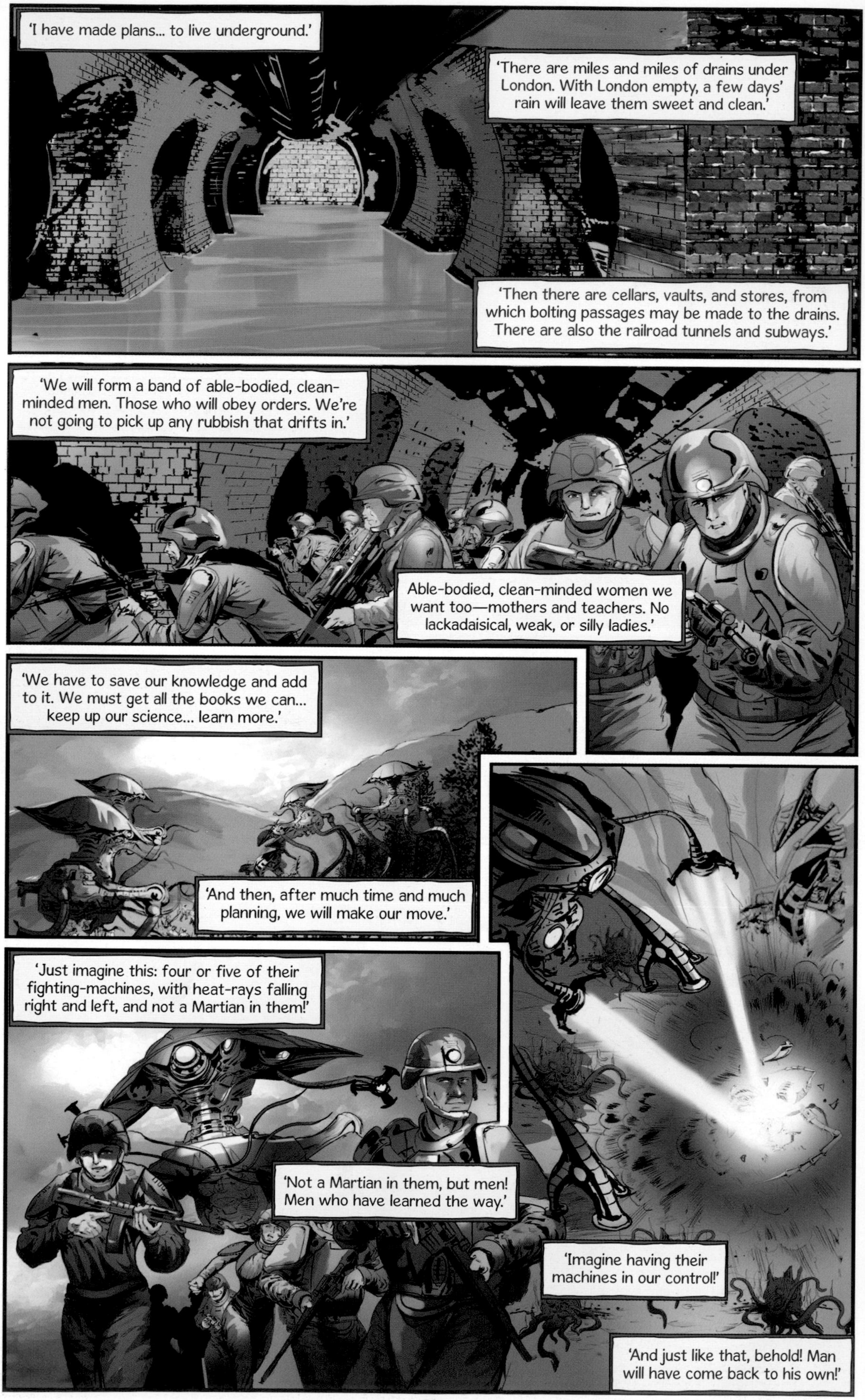
'I have made plans... to live underground.'
'There are miles and miles of drains under London. With London empty, a few days' rain will leave them sweet and clean.'
'Then there are cellars, vaults, and stores, from which bolting passages may be made to the drains. There are also the railroad tunnels and subways.'
'We will form a band of able-bodied, clean-minded men. Those who will obey orders. We're not going to pick up any rubbish that drifts in.'
Able-bodied, clean-minded women we want too—mothers and teachers. No lackadaisical, weak, or silly ladies.'
'We have to save our knowledge and add to it. We must get all the books we can... keep up our science... learn more.'
'And then, after much time and much planning, we will make our move.'
'Just imagine this: four or five of their fighting-machines, with heat-rays falling right and left, and not a Martian in them!'
'Not a Martian in them, but men! Men who have learned the way.'
'Imagine having their machines in our control!'
'And just like that, behold! Man will have come back to his own!'

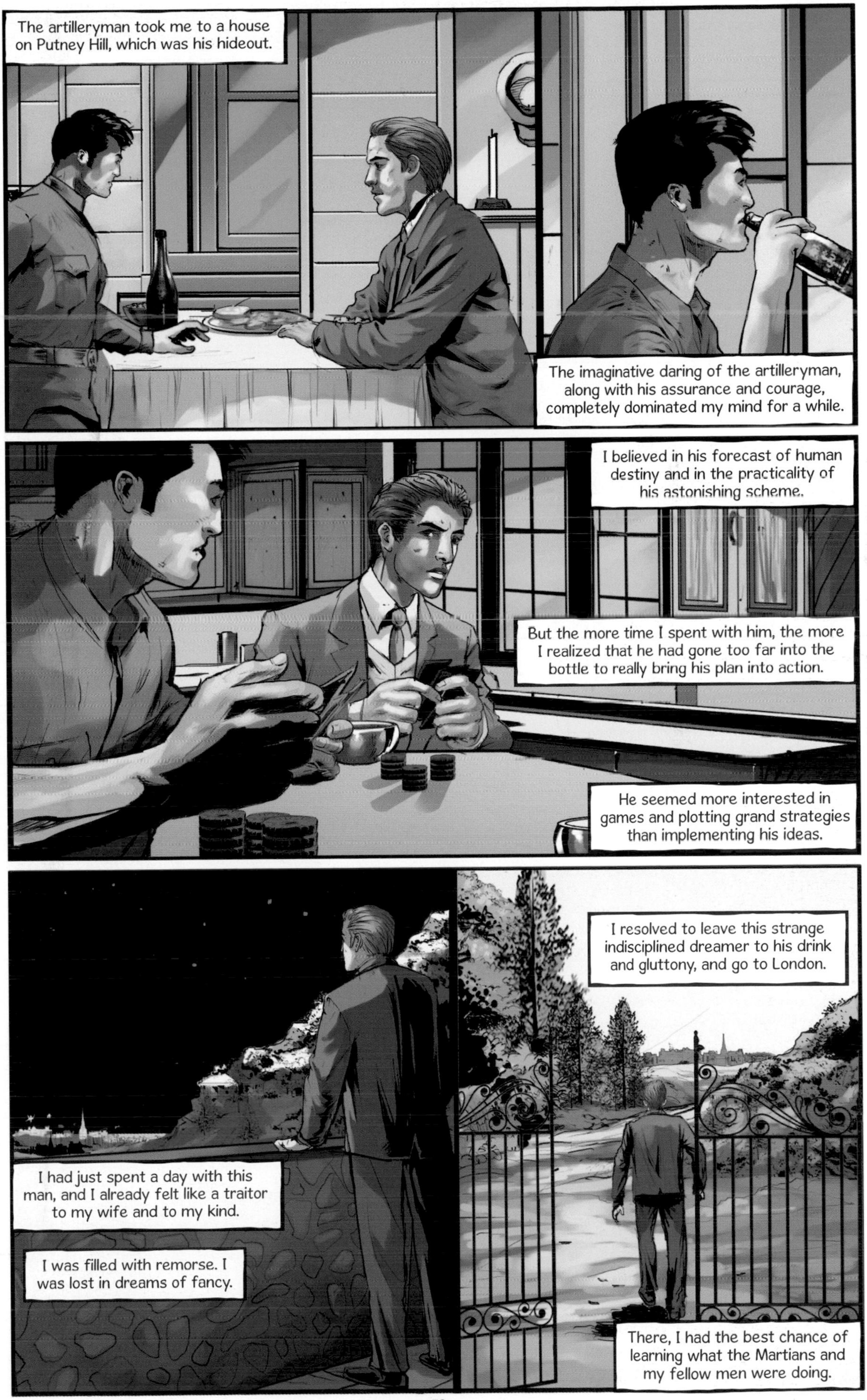
The artilleryman took me to a house on Putney Hill, which was his hideout.
The imaginative daring of the artilleryman, along with his assurance and courage, completely dominated my mind for a while.
I believed in his forecast of human destiny and in the practicality of his astonishing scheme.
But the more time I spent with him, the more I realized that he had gone too far into the bottle to really bring his plan into action.
He seemed more interested in games and plotting grand strategies than implementing his ideas.
I had just spent a day with this man, and I already felt like a traitor to my wife and to my kind.
I was filled with remorse. I was lost in dreams of fancy.
I resolved to leave this strange indisciplined dreamer to his drink and gluttony, and go to London.
There, I had the best chance of learning what the Martians and my fellow men were doing.

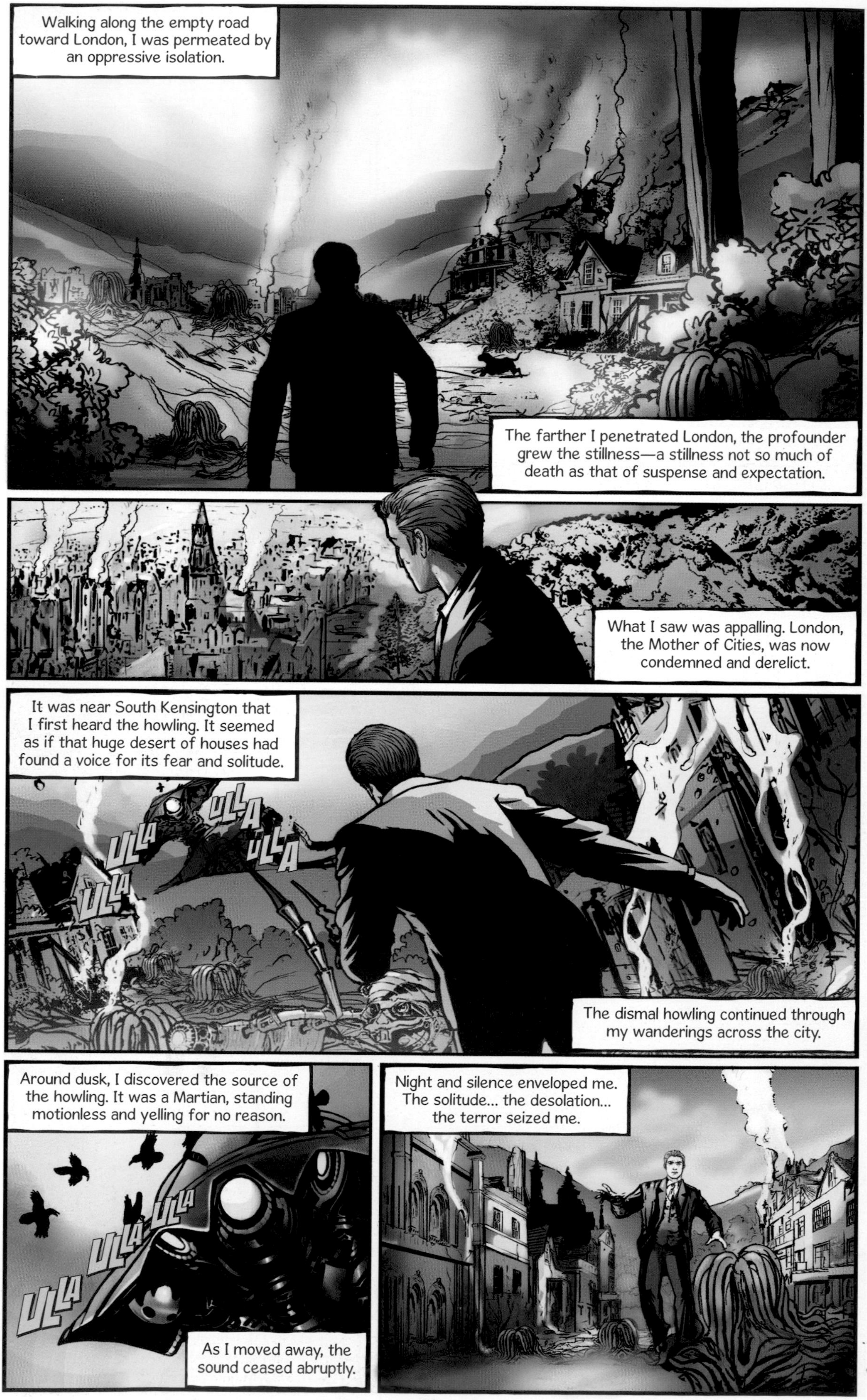
Walking along the empty road toward London, I was permeated by an oppressive isolation.
The farther I penetrated London, the profounder grew the stillness—a stillness not so much of death as that of suspense and expectation.
What I saw was appalling. London, the Mother of Cities, was now condemned and derelict.
It was near South Kensington that I first heard the howling. It seemed as if that huge desert of houses had found a voice for its fear and solitude.
ULLA
ULLA
ULLA
ULLA
The dismal howling continued through my wanderings across the city.
Around dusk, I discovered the source of the howling. It was a Martian, standing motionless and yelling for no reason.
ULLA
ULLA
ULLA
ULLA
As I moved away, the sound ceased abruptly.
Night and silence enveloped me. The solitude... the desolation... the terror seized me.

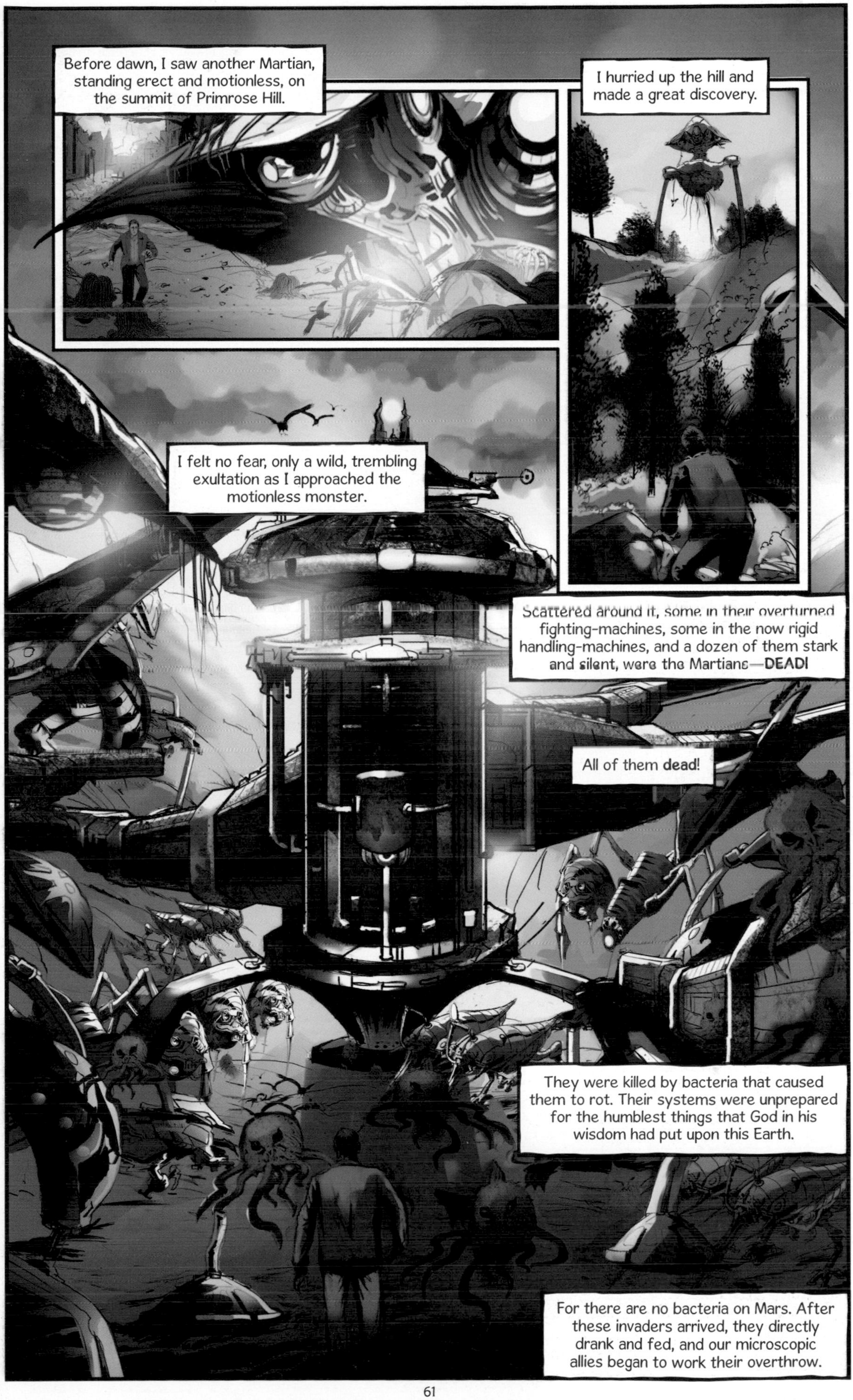
Before dawn, I saw another Martian, standing erect and motionless, on the summit of Primrose Hill.
I hurried up the hill and made a great discovery.
I felt no fear, only a wild, trembling exultation as I approached the motionless monster.
Scattered around it, some in their overturned fighting-machines, some in the now rigid handling-machines, and a dozen of them stark and silent, were the Martians—**DEAD!**
All of them **dead!**
They were killed by bacteria that caused them to rot. Their systems were unprepared for the humblest things that God in his wisdom had put upon this Earth.
For there are no bacteria on Mars. After these invaders arrived, they directly drank and fed, and our microscopic allies began to work their overthrow.

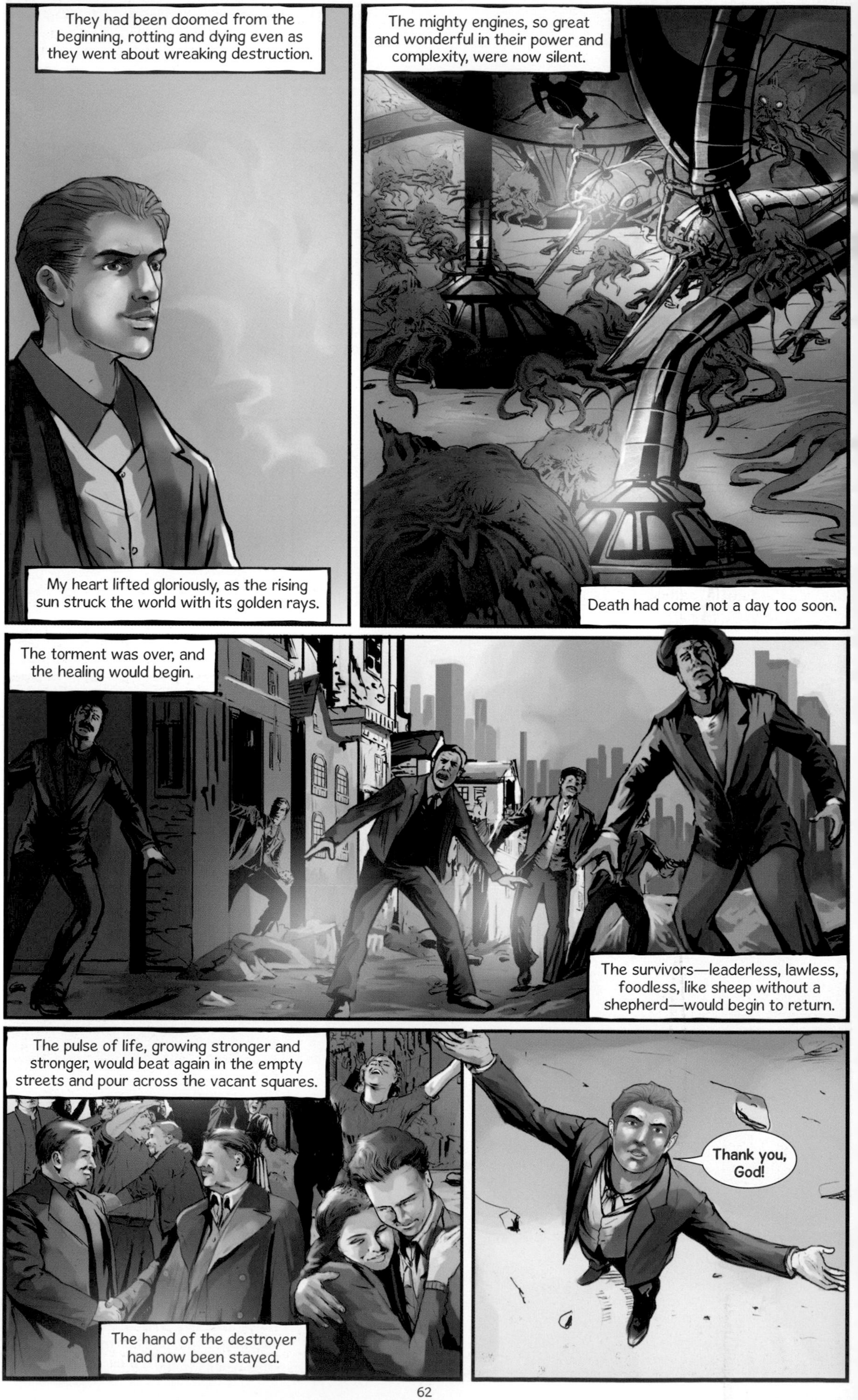
They had been doomed from the beginning, rotting and dying even as they went about wreaking destruction.
My heart lifted gloriously, as the rising sun struck the world with its golden rays.
The mighty engines, so great and wonderful in their power and complexity, were now silent.
Death had come not a day too soon.
The torment was over, and the healing would begin.
The survivors—leaderless, lawless, foodless, like sheep without a shepherd—would begin to return.
The pulse of life, growing stronger and stronger, would beat again in the empty streets and pour across the vacant squares.
The hand of the destroyer had now been stayed.
Thank you, God!

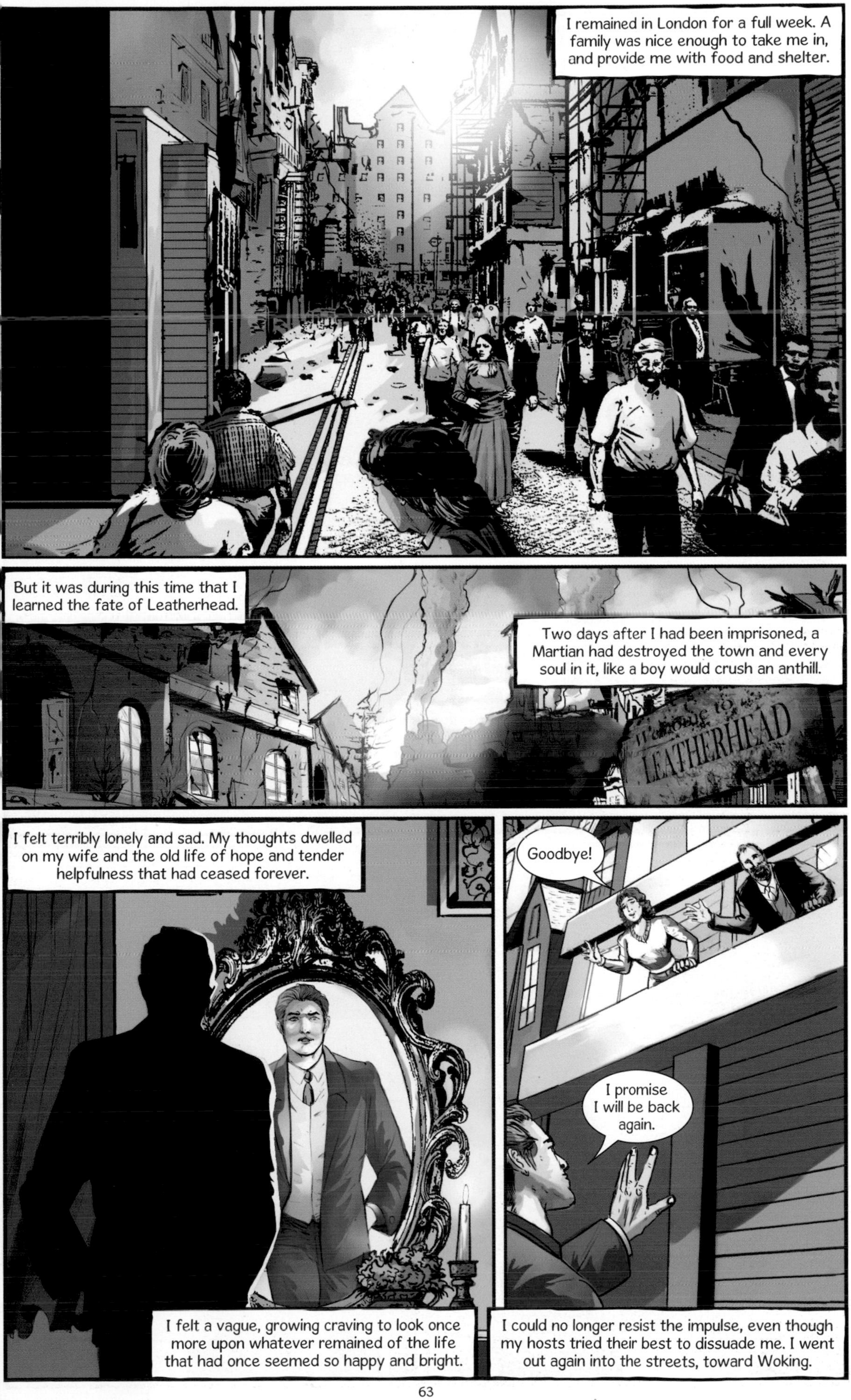
I remained in London for a full week. A family was nice enough to take me in, and provide me with food and shelter.
But it was during this time that I learned the fate of Leatherhead.
Two days after I had been imprisoned, a Martian had destroyed the town and every soul in it, like a boy would crush an anthill.
LEATHERHEAD
I felt terribly lonely and sad. My thoughts dwelled on my wife and the old life of hope and tender helpfulness that had ceased forever.
I felt a vague, growing craving to look once more upon whatever remained of the life that had once seemed so happy and bright.
Goodbye!
I promise I will be back again.
I could no longer resist the impulse, even though my hosts tried their best to dissuade me. I went out again into the streets, toward Woking.

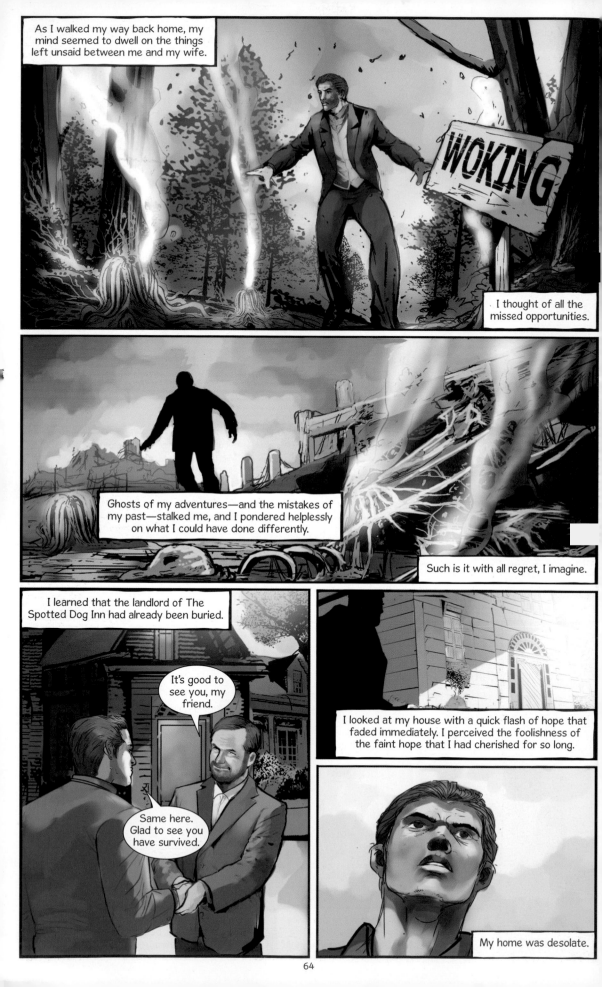

As I walked my way back home, my mind seemed to dwell on the things left unsaid between me and my wife.

I thought of all the missed opportunities.

Ghosts of my adventures—and the mistakes of my past—stalked me, and I pondered helplessly on what I could have done differently.

Such is it with all regret, I imagine.

I learned that the landlord of The Spotted Dog Inn had already been buried.

It's good to see you, my friend.

Same here. Glad to see you have survived.

I looked at my house with a quick flash of hope that faded immediately. I perceived the foolishness of the faint hope that I had cherished for so long.

My home was desolate.

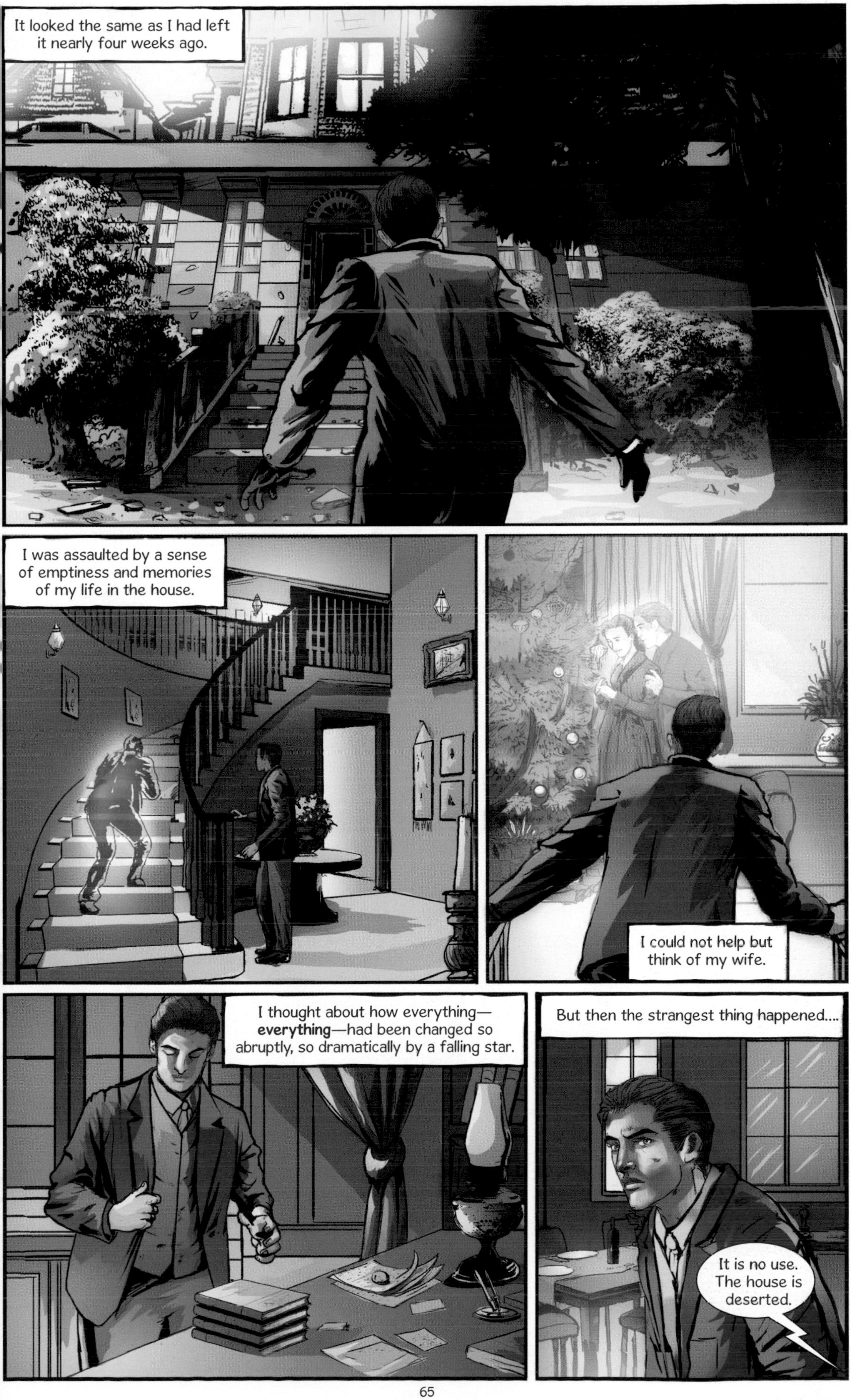
It looked the same as I had left it nearly four weeks ago.
I was assaulted by a sense of emptiness and memories of my life in the house.
I could not help but think of my wife.
I thought about how everything—**everything**—had been changed so abruptly, so dramatically by a falling star.
But then the strangest thing happened....
It is no use. The house is deserted.

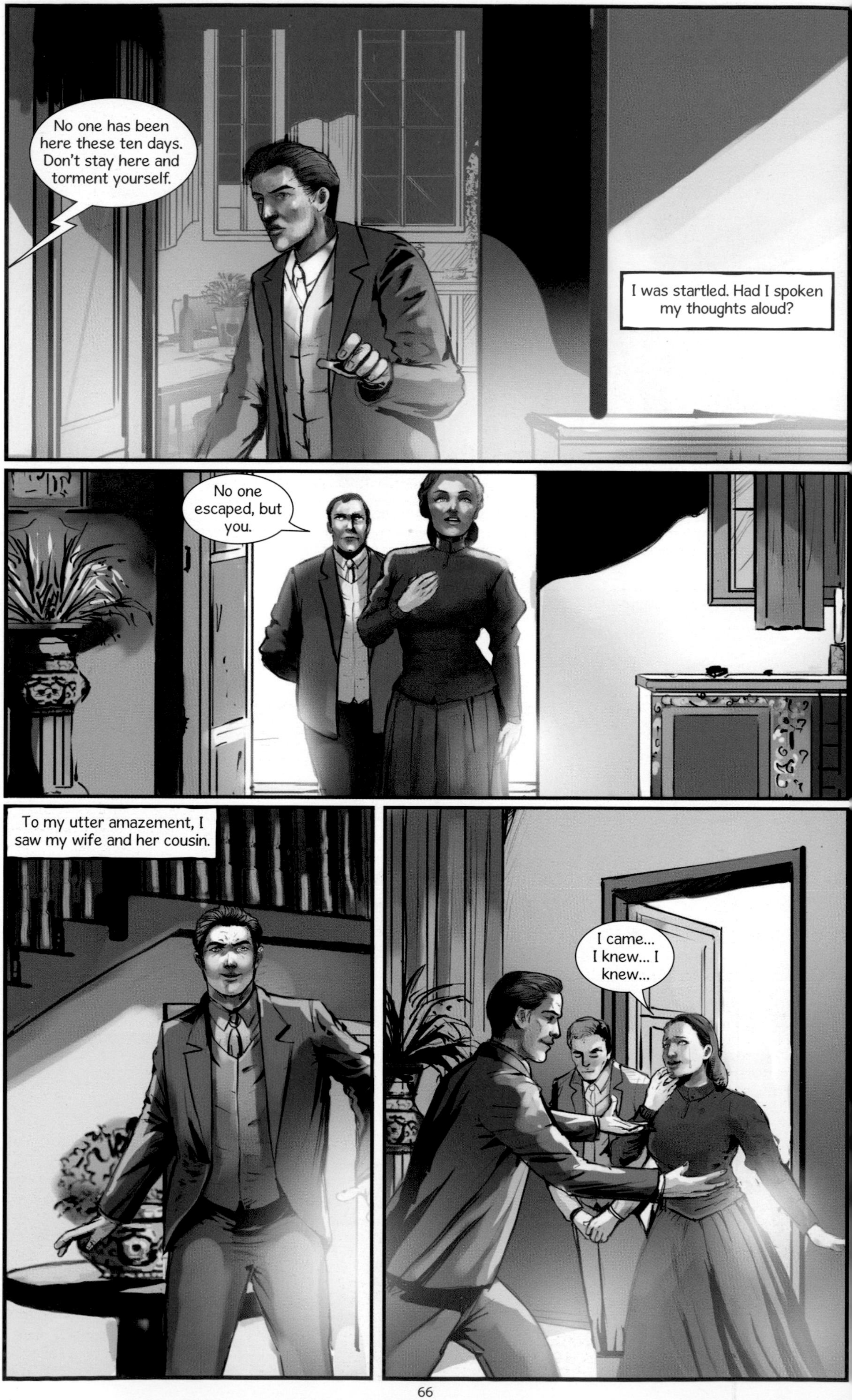
No one has been here these ten days. Don't stay here and torment yourself.
I was startled. Had I spoken my thoughts aloud?
No one escaped, but you.
To my utter amazement, I saw my wife and her cousin.
I came... I knew... I knew...

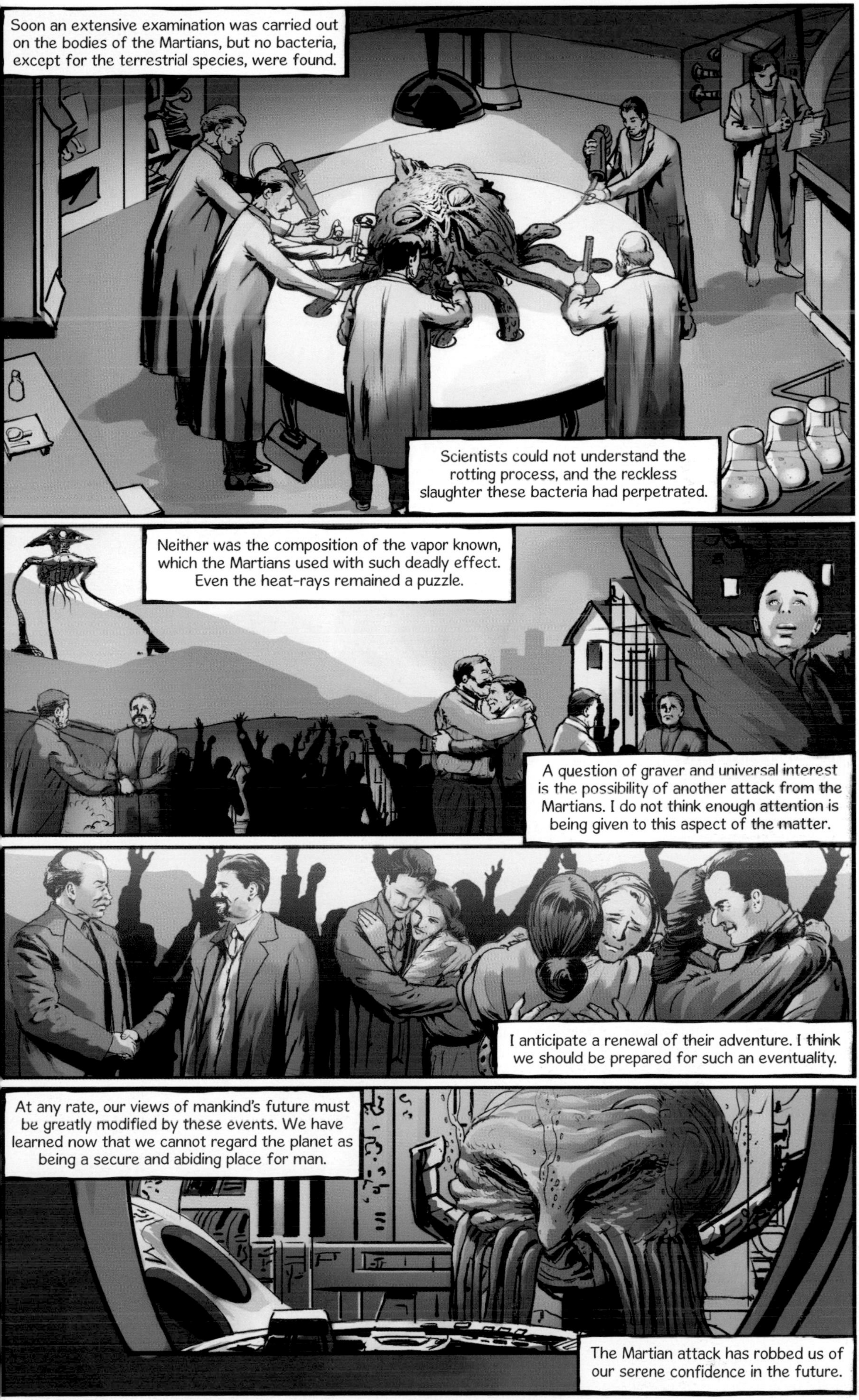
Soon an extensive examination was carried out on the bodies of the Martians, but no bacteria, except for the terrestrial species, were found.
Scientists could not understand the rotting process, and the reckless slaughter these bacteria had perpetrated.
Neither was the composition of the vapor known, which the Martians used with such deadly effect. Even the heat-rays remained a puzzle.
A question of graver and universal interest is the possibility of another attack from the Martians. I do not think enough attention is being given to this aspect of the matter.
I anticipate a renewal of their adventure. I think we should be prepared for such an eventuality.
At any rate, our views of mankind's future must be greatly modified by these events. We have learned now that we cannot regard the planet as being a secure and abiding place for man.
The Martian attack has robbed us of our serene confidence in the future.

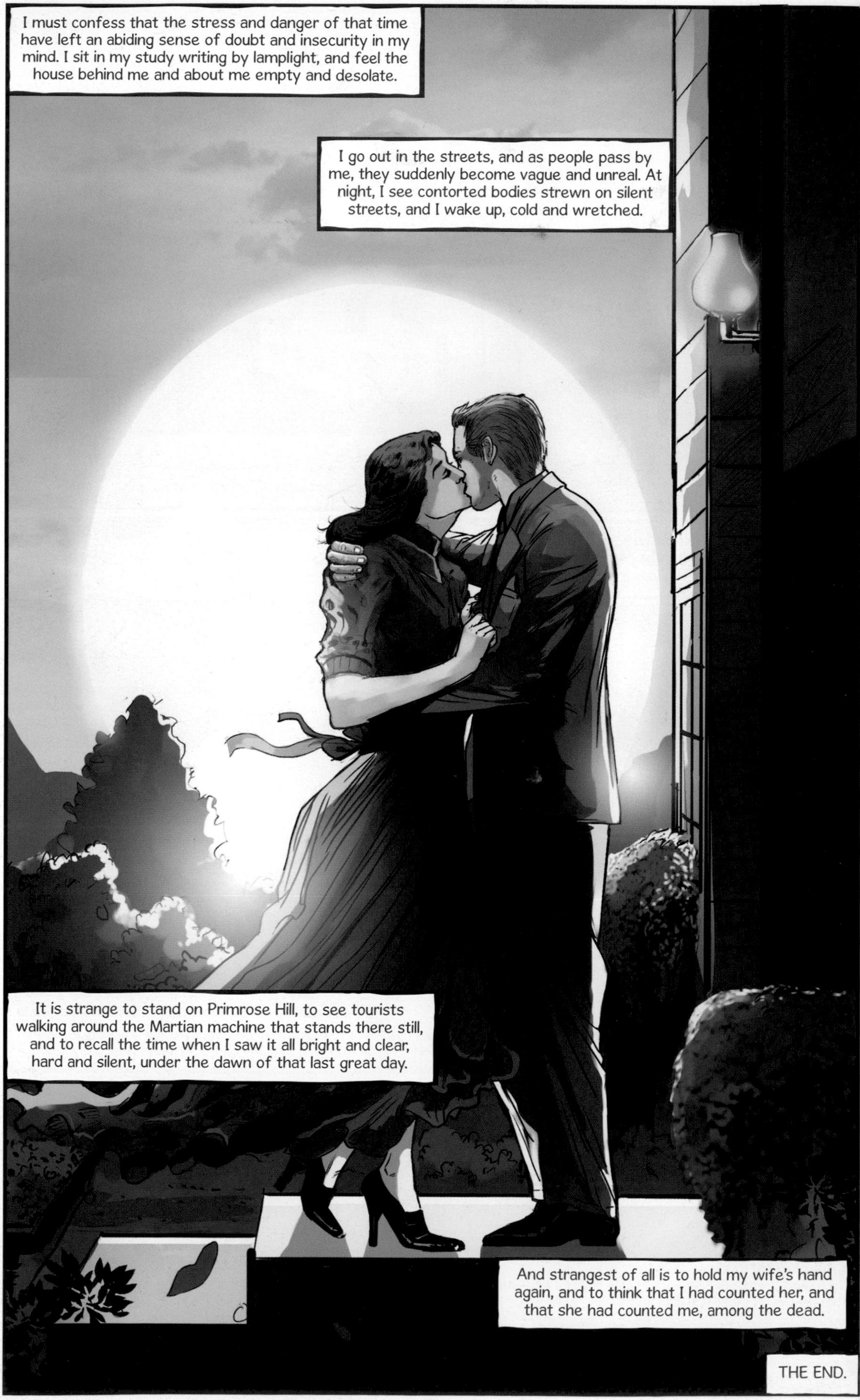
I must confess that the stress and danger of that time have left an abiding sense of doubt and insecurity in my mind. I sit in my study writing by lamplight, and feel the house behind me and about me empty and desolate.
I go out in the streets, and as people pass by me, they suddenly become vague and unreal. At night, I see contorted bodies strewn on silent streets, and I wake up, cold and wretched.
It is strange to stand on Primrose Hill, to see tourists walking around the Martian machine that stands there still, and to recall the time when I saw it all bright and clear, hard and silent, under the dawn of that last great day.
And strangest of all is to hold my wife's hand again, and to think that I had counted her, and that she had counted me, among the dead.
THE END.

SPACE RACE

Written by: C. E. L. Welsh
Illustrated by: K. L. Jones

CAMPFIRE
Originals
SPACE RACE
C. E. L. WELSH
ILLUSTRATED BY K. L. JONES

From gunpowder in ancient China, to inventions in Russia and the United States of America, the story of the Space Race is one that takes the reader all over the world... and beyond!

A substance from Earth that would carry man into space...

How did charcoal, one of the key ingredients of gunpowder, alter the course of warfare and make it possible for us to build giant structures in space?

This question and many more like it are answered in this thrilling historical story from Campfire.

Join Chet Riley and his grandfather as they relive the story of the Space Race—an event that was contested by the two greatest powers on Earth, and involved some of the most brilliant and inventive minds the world has ever seen.

Suitable for readers of all ages, *Space Race* combines beautiful artwork and a gripping story.

CCCP

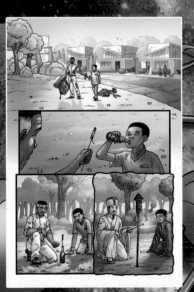

MYSTERIES OF THE WORLD

In ***The War of the Worlds***, aliens from Mars—Martians—attack Earth. Could H. G. Wells's novel be based on some element of truth? Could there be life on Mars? Is there intelligent life on other planets, and do aliens come to visit our planet once in a while? Read on to know some mind-boggling information on UFO (unidentified flying objects) sightings, strange happenings, and the ever-intriguing planet Mars.

UFO SIGHTING

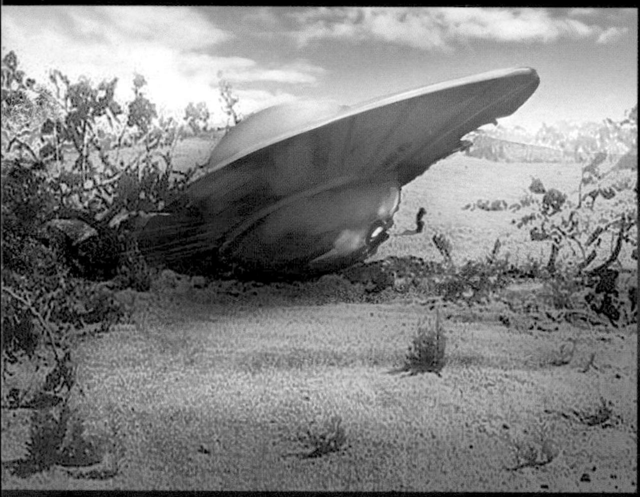

In 1987, while clicking photographs of the Ilkley Moor in England, Philip Spencer heard a humming sound. He turned around to see a small green creature, around four feet tall. According to Spencer, the creature moved away quickly, and when Spencer shouted, it turned and waved an arm dismissively. Spencer immediately took a photograph. Spencer followed the creature and saw a huge silver saucer disappear into the clouds. Apparently, the humming sound was from the saucer. Spencer lost more than two hours of his time and his compass also went haywire. The picture was shown to a UFO researcher and investigations started. Wildlife photography experts and Kodak laboratories revealed that the green creature was no animal and that the saucer was actually part of the photo and not superimposed!

CROP CIRCLES

Crop circles are mysterious formations found in crop fields. The crop is found flattened in intricate patterns that weren't there the previous day. No one has yet been able to explain how they are created.

The stalks within the circle are not broken. They are just bent a few centimeters above the ground, which lets them continue to grow horizontally. No tracks are found leading into or out of a crop circle pattern, and the earth beneath is undisturbed! Investigators have detected strong energy fields in such an area, and many eyewitnesses have sighted UFOs or strange lights in the sky in the surrounding areas where these crop circles are later found.

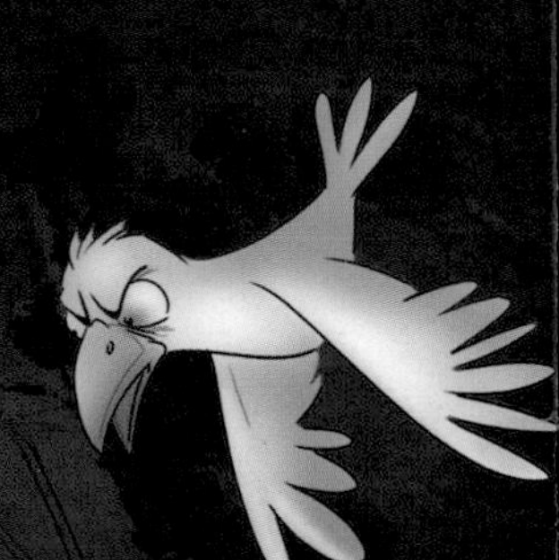

What's even stranger?

Inside crop circles:

- Birds alter their flight path!
- Cameras stop working, and batteries lose their charge!

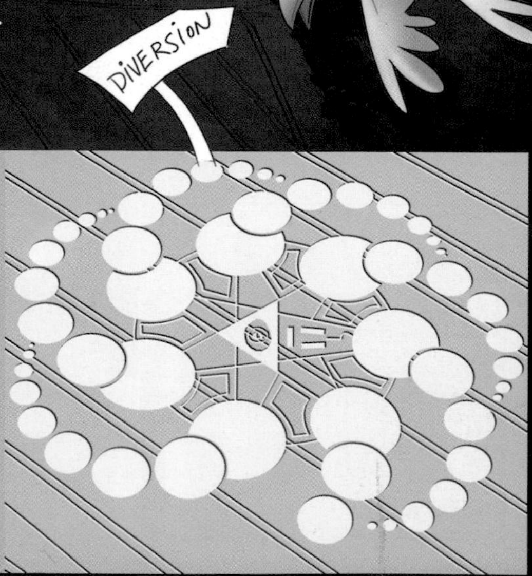
DIVERSION

MYSTERIOUS MARS

This famous planet, named after the Roman god of war, is the one that we earthlings are most fascinated with. In the 1880s, telescopes revealed strange markings on Mars which convinced people that Mars had canals built by an alien race!

Since the 1960s, many space missions have provided scientists with loads of interesting information. Currently, an ongoing robotic space mission by NASA (National Aeronautics and Space Administration) has sent two rovers—unmanned remote-controlled vehicles used to carry out scientific research—named Spirit and Opportunity to explore Mars.

OPPORTUNITY

SPIRIT

HERE ARE SOME MORE INTERESTING FACTS ABOUT THE RED PLANET:

Mars has the largest mountain in the Solar System! Olympus Mons on Mars rises a full 24 km above its surrounding plain. Its base is more than 500 km across and is framed by a 6-km high cliff! That makes Mount Everest—roughly 8.85 km tall—look like a pimple!

The largest canyon in Mars makes the Grand Canyon look tiny! Valles Marineris, a network of canyons on Mars, runs 4000 km long and stands from 2 to 7 km tall while the Grand Canyon is just about 446 km long and 1.83 km tall.

Water on Mars? Though there is no water on Mars now, scientists claim that large lakes or even oceans might have once existed on this planet. Clear evidence of water erosion can be seen in old river channels and floodplains. It seems that water existed long ago, but only for a very short while.

DID YOU KNOW?

- A 1938 radio broadcast of *The War of the Worlds* in U.S.A. scared millions of listeners into believing that aliens from Mars were actually coming to attack Earth! It resulted in a mass panic attack amongst listeners!

- A 23-feet high sculpture of a tripod fighting machine, called 'The Martian', based on the description of Martian fighting machines in the novel, stands near the railroad station in Woking, England.

Available now

Putting the fun back into reading

Explore the latest from Campfire at

www.campfire.co.in